GIDEON'S CONFESSION

GIDEON'S CONFESSION

JOSEPH G. PETERSON

SWITCHGRASS BOOKS   NORTHERN ILLINOIS UNIVERSITY PRESS   DeKalb

© 2014 by Joseph G. Peterson

Published by Switchgrass Books; the Northern Illinois
University Press, DeKalb, Illinois 60115

Manufactured in the United States using acid-free paper

All Rights Reserved

Design by Shaun Allshouse

Library of Congress Cataloging in Publication Data
Peterson, Joseph G.
Gideon's confession / Joseph G. Peterson.
paged cm
ISBN 978-0-87580-702-7 (pbk) —
 ISBN 978-1-60909-161-3 (e-book)
1. Losers—Fiction. 2. Single men—Fiction.
3. Uncles—Fiction. I. Title.
PS3616.E84288G53 2014
813'.6—dc23
2013045650

For my mom and dad, who taught me dis and dat

Before my uncle died his checks arrived in the mail the first Wednesday of every month. I don't know why they arrived, but they arrived nonetheless, like a benediction.

The first check came in the mail when I was nineteen years old, and I had no idea then that more checks would come, but come they did with unfailing regularity until the final check, which arrived six months after he had passed away. It arrived exactly on my twenty-ninth birthday with a little note that spoke from the grave. It said, merely: This is the end of them.

During the time he sent the checks I received little raises every six months or so, what my uncle called "cost of living increases," and they were designed to keep pace with something he intuited all himself: my growing needs. With his monthly checks he usually appended a small note asking how I was doing, and I usually sent a small reply thanking him, letting him know that everything was fine.

In his notes, which were tidily handwritten with an ink pen, he would divulge the particulars of his month with an epistolary formality that reminded me of a pen pal relationship I had carried on during my grammar school days with a Belgium boy named Berndt. Berndt was always striving to hit a more intimate note with me, but distance, the language barrier, and of course the fact that we never actually met prevented him from doing so. What's more, I remained habitually coy with him— always responding to his missives, never initiating a round of my own. With my uncle it was the same way. I sensed he wanted a more confessional relationship with me, only he didn't know how to confess—having been born in the teens and spent his early manhood in the Depression. Hell, he still believed in the honor code. Which honor code was that? Suffice it to say he'd do the standard thirty paces by the book and go down in a duel if he had to. As a result he hadn't learned the language of our talk show era: the confessional. He had too much dignity to split himself open and talk. He'd rather die. What's more, he had this epistolary habit, which I've noticed in people of his generation, of omitting the first person pronoun, and the effect is a sort of shorthand that, in this era of Me, reads shockingly like self-erasure. A typical note reads as follows:

> Went with Nan to doc. Found bumps on thyroid. Nothing serious. Lost eighty same day at greyhounds when dog took lead in fourth turn and blew his heart. Advise you, son, to stay away from gambling—dogs in particular. Went to Club Saturday night and discussed your dilemma with friends. They all recommend a career in banking. Would send more info on subject if you're interested. Got drunk Sunday aft. on a new drink, The Hurricano. Have you heard of it? Spent all Monday morning recuperating and golfed a desultory nine in the afternoon. What else is new? Lost thirty Tuesday at Bingo. Nan made it up with $100 earning. Today back with Nan to doc for more tests. Enclosed a little something. Hope it holds you over till next month. Love always, Unc.

A typical response from me might read:

> Thanks, Unc. for the check. I've deposited it, so you can balance your books. Everything is going good—GOOD!—and I'm looking for a job. All in all, I'm doing my best. Love, Gideon

My uncle was everything I wished my father had been. He was supportive, funny, nonjudgmental. What's more, he smiled on my progress, which is something my father has never done. My father doesn't believe I've made any progress at all. He thinks I'm doomed to eternal failure. He thinks I'm untrustworthy, unreliable, and if he doesn't think I'm exactly dishonest, he has a deep suspicion that I'm capable of grave moral turpitude and mendacity. A favorite word of his, mendacity. The mendacity, he liked to scream, echoing a famous play. The mendacity! He refuses to talk to me as a result. I tried to talk to him during those years, but he'd put his hand up and frown. Please, Gideon. You had your chance—it's time to move on.

I don't know what chance he was talking about. Perhaps he was referring to the fact that I had spent my childhood under his roof with my two brothers. They had their chance as well, but he was still talking to them. Apparently, my chance had come and gone. It was all water under the bridge; things between him and me had irrevocably washed away.

But my uncle! What more could a nephew ask for? I have a picture of him I keep in my wallet. The date of the photo typed in minute red ink, 1973, is still visible on the white border of the picture. I was eight years old when it was taken. He had flown in to see me receive my First Communion. He was, among other things, my godfather—and after the festivities surrounding my communion were over, he took me to Chicago. I grew up in Wheeling, Illinois, a north suburb of Chicago, and, though I was only a half hour away from downtown, I may as well have been, for all intents and purposes (we never visited it), a lifetime away. So he took me to the tourist sites, such as he conceived of them. We saw the Marina Towers that stood towering like two beehives over the Chicago River. We walked over to the Wrigley Building half-hoping we might obtain some gum, and failing that, we went to the top of the John Hancock, which, at the time, had just been squeezed out by the Sears Tower as the tallest building. We stared down from those still staggering heights on all the people as if they were ants. He told me that if I dropped a penny from where I stood and hit one of those human ants in the head it would penetrate that person like a bullet—go straight through him and imbed itself into the concrete sidewalk. Such a fact amazed me. Then he told me to hold a penny in my hand—which I did—and, gently tapping my head, he told me: There's an object lesson here for you, son. There's power in small change!

My uncle took me to lunch at the Berghoff where we ate roasted goose, cranberry sauce with real cranberries and stuffed ourselves full of schnitzel. I remember going around with him on the subway eating a bag of Brach's red-hot candy. They were small little heart-shaped candies that stained your palms red. They burned my tongue. I loved them. I couldn't eat enough of them, and you can see the tips of my fingers, even in the picture, stained by red dye number 2. There he is standing next to me. We're at the Museum of Science and Industry in front of the U-505 sub. I'm a small little tyke, and he's not too big himself, just over five feet. My uncle had been a sailor on a destroyer escort ship, the *Jenks*, during World War II, and he was proud as hell to tell me how his boat had taken the U-505 off the coast of Mauritania. He later became friends with one of the captured crewmen from the U-boat. The U-boater's name was Horst. Horst had been a Nazi POW in a camp in Canada, and later, after the war and seeing Germany's devastation, he moved to Chicago's South Side where he started a small concern manufacturing manhole covers. My uncle told me all about it: how he and Horst had met by accident at Disney World—outside the ride It's a Small Small World—how they swapped addresses, and how they maintained, until I entered into the picture, a respectful epistolary friendship. I wish I had a collection of those letters.

ONE SUMMER MY UNCLE had gotten me a job at the mill where they manufactured those manhole covers. It was to tide me over until I found a suitable job—one rising to the level of my education. Despite the fact that my uncle recommended me for the job, I received no special dispensation from Horst, who remained aloof from the rest of the mill workers. Except for the comment he made to me that he had come over from Germany to America because the streets were paved with gold, a comment to which, by the way, I unexpectedly laughed, he remained aloof from me as well. He stayed in his office going over papers and answering the telephone.

My job was to clean a milling machine that had gone to seed. It was a vast machine with all sorts of intricate, hard-to-reach places. It had received several coats of paint over the decades, and paint chips, as well as dirt, metal shavings, and other detritus caked the entire machine. I was required to squat uncomfortably in the desolate warehouse space and, with a toothbrush in hand as well as a towel, some metal scrub pads, and a solvent, clean the machine and bring it up to snuff. It was terrible, unpleasant work. Doubly terrible because it put me in mind of my father who, I'm sure, would have felt pleased to see me do such work. I wished he and I could be closer, but such things weren't meant to be. I scrubbed the machine best I could, and at night when I came home, I blew my nose and it came out black. It wasn't until summer's end when Horst paid me a visit. He was a short, broadly built man. He leaned on a cane as he walked, and when he came through the door of the old warehouse building and saw how I had transformed the milling machine from a dirty wreck to a splendidly clean wreck, he gave a little snort of pleasure.

Anderson, he said, calling me by my last name.

Yes, sir.

I will tell your uncle you do good work. He spoke with a thick German accent.

Thank you, sir, I said.

It's nigger work, Anderson, he said. But your uncle told me not to spare you.

Thanks again, I said humbly. I appreciate the opportunity.

Most manufacturers wouldn't go through the trouble of cleaning this machine. But we don't waste a thing here.

I found a rag and was wiping my hands.

Your uncle is a good man even though he sank my boat. Now we write letters back and forth and talk about the war.

He never mentions his war experience to me, I said.

Oh, he is a great reminiscer. Only problem—he sides with the Jews.

I remained silent.

Those Jews, he said, bitterly. They cry. They cry. But if Hitler had done his job right, we would not have to hear them cry so much. You tell your uncle that when you talk to him.

I wasn't aware they were crying.

That is because you do not listen! Your uncle doesn't either, for that matter.

He clicked his cane, made a little snort: God's chosen people! He turned and marched out of the empty warehouse. It was the last I saw of him.

When I later told my uncle of this unsavory conversation, he expressed regret that he had put me in harm's way. He sent me a letter of apology and a check for $400. Like that, I was on the gravy train.

MY UNCLE WAS VERY GENEROUS with his money. I can't complain. A lot of it came my way during those years. Implicit with his checks was the hope that I would voluntarily wean myself from them. My uncle used to suggest that it might be helpful if I put together a plan of what I thought I might want to accomplish in life. Coming from the Depression Era, he was a very practical man. For him, a plan was a beginning. It was a start. My plan would set me on my way to a life of accomplishment.

He wished I would put together a two- or three-page memo outlining my goals with a plan for how I hoped to obtain those goals. He told me time and again, it was OK if my plan was provisional. You should be thinking of the future but not be bound by it, he would advise time to time. If you're unsure or unwilling to commit to anything right now, don't worry. Just put something—a workable plan—together and send it to me. I'm interested to see where you're at.

The wonder of my uncle is that he was so open-minded and forgiving. He understood that in a world of options picking just one thing to commit head and heart to wouldn't be easy. On the other hand there was always that threat if I didn't put a plan together soon, he'd have to pull his funding. You have to understand, Gideon, he wrote in more than a few of his letters during this period, I can't go on writing these checks if you can't produce for me that little plan we talked about. Without such a plan, the money will have to be, ipso facto finito. It's only reasonable.

He used those words exactly: ipso facto finito. He had been a successful lawyer after all, and he liked to pepper his speech with legalisms. And in truth, he was right: it was reasonable.

TO BE HONEST (and what is the purpose of a confessional but to be honest) I used to worry about the prospect of being cut off. Oh on the surface I tried to be nonchalant about the whole matter. Calm, cool, and collected. I expressed my nonchalance in curious ways—by being a spendthrift for one. I pretended I liked to shop even though I hated it. Compulsively and often on a whim,

I would go on shopping sprees with my uncle's money. I loved to purchase gifts for friends and, of course, for myself. Occasionally I needed to cure myself of an inexplicable sadness, and I would do so by buying myself something useless and precious. For example, I bought several gorgeous hand-stamped leather albums with plastic inserts for my baseball card collection, which I had put together by chewing countless sticks of Topps gum. The plan for this purchase was that it would force me to sort out my cards from five or six shoeboxes. I would create nine positions for each sheet of plastic lining, and I would fill in players from the same team in their respective positions. In this way, I would be able to judge the strengths and weaknesses of my collection. So I bought the plastic inserts, the embossed leather albums that the inserts would slide into. I purchased scissors, paper, stick glue, and some other craft materials, and I spent a whole weekend pouring over my collection attempting to sort it out, but while I was working on the project I quickly realized it was ill-conceived because each pouch in the plastic liners only held a card or two, and for some teams I had piles of third basemen but only one or two catchers—and the whole thing was uneven. What's more, after I had sorted out my "prized" baseball card collection I noticed countless gaping omissions and useless repetitions, and it depressed me so much that I had to go off to the local bar for a drink and cool off.

The point is, I would be motivated for a shopping spree. A feeling would overtake me: I'd want to purchase something to signify that I had buying power, and I'd proceed to buy useless stuff. Another foolish item that I purchased during this time was something I had taken to by reading the advertisements in a magazine. I fell for a product called The Bone Fone. It was an AM/FM music radio device that fit in a blue socklike sleeve. The innovation of this product was that it wrapped around the shoulders like a scarf and sat on the collarbone emitting music. The idea was that it would emit music directly into the collarbone. No one else would hear the device but the user who would hear the music resonating through his bones more clearly than if the music had been heard by the ears. When I saw the ad for this thing, which was wrapped around the shoulders of a busty model in a tight T-shirt, I knew I needed to have it, and when I purchased it for $69.95 and used it for a few hours I realized that the damned thing—a piece of junk—didn't work and that I'd been hoodwinked by a good piece of advertisement. That being said, I had purchased it with my uncle's money, and for a moment, while anticipating the delivery of The Bone Fone in the mail, I felt like I had accomplished something useful, if not soulful.

Shopping in this way for useless things became for me a way of getting things done. The more useless the thing the better, I suppose. As a result I have a collection of tchotchkes—souvenirs that now sit uselessly collecting dust in the perpetual night of a storage locker kept deep in the bowels of my building. A partial list of other items collected in this way: a half-dozen or so balsa-wood airplanes that I had brought to various states of incompletion (but none to the final state of wrapping the plane in the special tissue paper and applying the butyrate dope to harden the tissue) and returned to their respective boxes for a later date when I would have the patience, in addition to the time, to finish them; a handful of silk vests that I had purchased in the remarkable hope of radically altering my persona in one fell swoop, but I can't remember why I didn't have the courage to follow through on such a sartorial switcheroo; and an intact beer-can collection of 100 cans of beer all collected in the 1950s by an old man named Vern (who dyed his thick head of hair yellow) whom I had met at a flea market. I would show friends this rusting collection, and I'd emphatically point out that they were cans. Do you hear that, I would say, tapping on the metal with my fingernail. They are not aluminum, like the cans of today, but unbendable steel! The stuff skyscrapers, ships, and America are built upon! I also purchased a mock-ivory grooming set that included shoehorns, combs, brushes, toenail and fingernail clippers and files, nose-hair trimmers, mustache and whisker electric shaving devices, and scissors. I kept myself groomed at the local barber who never charged more than $10 for a cut, and I shaved with a razor. What's more, I wore gym shoes and so I was never in need of shoehorns, but I purchased the set because it was beautiful in its uselessness, and I set it aside for a later date when a different me might need these items. I also purchased a couple of exercise machines (a Nordic Track cross-country ski machine; a rowing machine), and among the crazier health improvement items I purchased but never used were a canister of vitamins and a "vibrating belt" that was designed to help me melt fat—effortlessly—from my midsection. All of these things—or rather all of this garbage—GARBAGE—was purchased with my uncle's money and with some hope that a future me would not only find a use for the stuff but that that self would also be molded by these items. Needless to say, that future self never emerged, and the items arrived in the mail: shiny, ready to perform their tasks, and I made them wait, quietly—uselessly—in the wings.

I also, and this is perhaps most unpardonable, thought nothing of giving handouts to anyone on the street corner who requested money to help him get by, or take a bus home, or take a train to some distant burgh far from Chicago. I fell victim to all sorts of capers and scams. I was a sentimentalist when it came to charity. I was a regular contributor to the Fraternal Order of Policeman's fund. (I supported this fund partly because I feared the police and worried what they might do to me if I should say no.) I gave money to Jerry Lewis's Muscular Dystrophy Association. I gave money to the Make-a-Wish Foundation. I gave money to the Ronald McDonald House. I gave money to Catholic Charities. I supported a group who was reseeding Illinois with prairie grasses. I gave to the Anti-Cruelty Society. I gave money to the NRA and to Green Peace. I gave money to public TV and public radio and the classical music station. I gave money to AIDS research. I watched football and signed checks to the United Way and on and on. None of my contributions were more than twenty dollars, but they were better than giving nothing. I would give to panhandlers I met on the street trying to sell me free circulars. You need money for a meal, pal? Here, get yourself something to eat. You need a drink or a fix to get high? Here, this one's on me. I gave and gave. What the hell, they're no different from me, so why shouldn't they receive a little of the help I receive? And so went my uncle's money.

Nevertheless, in the wee hours of the night my defenses would crumble, and I would find myself shaken to the core. I would lie awake and worry: what if the money were to suddenly dry up? What if my uncle Eddie should suddenly stop funding me? Wasn't all this spending a waste? Shouldn't it be put to a better use, like starting a savings account, for instance, or even investing in stocks and bonds? But I didn't know how to go about the elaborate business of getting set up with a broker. (What would it have taken—an afternoon perusing the phone book and a ten-minute phone call?) The late night worries would mount, the regret at waste would be all about, and then suddenly it would occur to me: Uncle Eddie's money won't go away. He's a veritable brick. No, he's not, my doubt would reassert—no one is absolutely reliable, not even good Uncle Eddie. Nevertheless, in the wee hours of the morning or in the late hours of the night, as the case may be, when I was suffering from insomnia or couldn't sleep on account of too much booze or nicotine or caffeine, I would suddenly begin to resemble that worrier in Michelangelo's *Last Judgment*—you know, the guy who worries, chewing his fingers off, dying of anxiety—because even if I should provide my uncle with a plan, he still might croak. It's not good believing he'll live forever, and if he dies, Nan, his second wife, will surely cut me off.

She and I have never gotten along. She's hated me from the first. We're of two different worlds. Oil and water. She despises the fact that I have a benefactor in her husband. Unlike me, she has never had a leg up on the world. She never got the benefit of the doubt (as I, no doubt, have). I've heard her complain about it: the hopelessness of her life before she met my uncle. She never went to college. Hell, she didn't finish high school. Instead she was pregnant at fifteen and off working in the service industry cleaning shitty little rooms in a motel underneath the highway. There were years of terror and depravity at every corner—her daughter drowned in a creek, and her raven-eaten body was discovered a week later by a dog. Then there was the temptation to end it all or succumb to drug addiction, alcohol, and welfare. Yet she hung in there cleaning those damned motel rooms while waiting . . . waiting for her luck to turn . . . waiting for my uncle to arrive.

He's no better than I am, she would say, pointing her finger at me. And yet, he gets the benefit of the doubt, a luxury I never had. Even his own father won't support him and why? Because he hasn't earned his father's trust. He has squandered everything his father ever gave him, and now he's off squandering this money you give him. Why do you do it, Eddie? Why do you support this boy?

I heard it too many times: the long harangue. Yet I always stood there, standing, I should say, taking her wrath, being screamed at by her in front of my benefactor. She, of course, was right, and I never disagreed with her. My father had abandoned me because I had squandered his trust, and I didn't deserve the help I got from my uncle, but the key thing is, I got my uncle's help nonetheless. And this fact, the fact of my uncle's help, is important. It rapidly became a fact of my life. I grew dependent on it and to some extent I was who I was partly because of it. If my uncle's money stopped coming, especially if it should stop abruptly, as I worried it would during those long nights, I'd be up the creek. I knew this, as did Nan.

As did my uncle. If his money stopped without warning, did I have Nan's inner resources to face years of terror and depravity? Absolutely not. Hell, the temptation to give up hope to alcohol and drugs was already nearly more than I could resist, and unlike her, I didn't have an explanation why this should be. More practically, I had bills that needed to be paid: credit card debt, college loans, and rent checks that I could ill afford not to pay. I didn't have any prospects for work. My experience at the manhole factory convinced me that I never again wanted to do a day's manual labor. I certainly didn't want to go through what Nan went through cleaning motel rooms. I'd rather die before stooping to that. But I had to do something. What, I couldn't say. Yet this is exactly what my uncle required of me back then: an answer to his question. What would I do, should the money run out? Of course, the thought also occurred to me, time to time, that if I did indeed get a job, then the flow of money from my uncle would naturally abate. And why would I? Why would a rational person do anything to cause a revenue stream—a free one at that—to dry up?

Perhaps—and this is an idea I had for a long time—I thought I might start a company that would manufacture windless umbrellas. It was an idea I had during a terrible storm, running down the street with my umbrella in hand when a wind caught my umbrella at the wrong angle and broke it at the stem. It occurred to me that a better umbrella could be designed: one with vents to let the wind through and perhaps flaps over the vents to keep the rain out. I would call it Anderson's Windless Umbrella. And my ad campaign would read: Buy Anderson's Windless Umbrellas and Be Blown Away. You'll

Never Need Another Umbrella Again—Ever! And It's Guaranteed!

At the time, it was the best I could do in terms of career planning, yet I never had the courage to send this idea to him for fear I would be laughed out of Dodge. Don't they already make this kind of umbrella, and how is yours different? What's more, when push came to shove I could see that getting this idea off the ground was infinitely more complex and difficult than I was capable of. After all, it isn't so easy to figure out how to go from a simple idea to a whole manufacturing process. Horst, unsavory though he may be, could evidently do it, as could a host of others, but not I. I don't know what prevented me from trying. A lack of will? Boredom? Or the terrible sense that I wouldn't even know where or how to begin?

WHENEVER I WOKE in the morning from a night of worrying, I would step forth into the precious light of day, and I'd be inexplicably reassured: my uncle's checks will never stop coming. He'll never cut me off. We're tied at the hip—even if his is an artificial implant. As to his health, he's strong as an ox! He was my mother's brother, and he was fond of saying our kind lives forever. As a result of such thinking—what I call daytime thinking—I was little motivated to develop the plan he required. Whenever I settled down to do it, something always diverted my attention: NASCAR racing on TV or an NCAA basketball playoff I couldn't miss or a telephone call from an old friend who wanted to meet me for a drink at the tavern.

But my uncle persisted. He started to advise me quite sensibly to see a career counselor. If you're having trouble figuring out what to do with your life, visit the career center at your alma mater. I'm sure they can help. Later he asked if I had done as he advised, and I told him I had. Were the counselors helpful? he asked.

Quite, I lied.

Wonderful. I look forward to seeing your plan soon.

When my plan wasn't immediately forthcoming (immediately being several months) I received a package from him in the mail. I opened it up, wondering what it could be. Packages always thrill me, especially packages from my uncle. I peeled the wrap away and was suddenly disappointed to see he had sent me *What Color Is Your Parachute?* I opened it up to see if there was a check inside. A little note fell out instead. Nan recommended to send you this. You might read it for some ideas.

I threw the book across the room. I was furious. If it came from Nan, I was really worried. So she's the one putting him up to this. Nevertheless, after I had calmed down, I decided to try and read the book, lest—heaven forbid—I be quizzed on it. Then, after spending an hour or two on it, I discovered it was crammed with religious preaching. I threw it in the garbage.

I went down to the tavern and spent the rest of a Sunday afternoon watching NASCAR. The cars going round and round, droningly. Keeping an eye out for accidents. Just like life. Victor—the elderly gentleman who tends the bar and who means the world to me— knew I was stewing about something so he stayed away. I was already on my sixth beer when a guy walked into the bar. For a moment I thought it might be Walt, but I was drunk at that point, and I probably needed my eyes checked, because instead of Walt it was a clean-cut guy in a business suit. I thought he looked decent enough. Either that or I was in desperate need of company, so I offered him the barstool next to me and bought him a beer. We started talking about this and that. He said he was from out of town—Madison, Wisconsin. What brings you here? I asked.

Would you believe a funeral?

And yes, yes I would believe it. Folks are always coming in here mourning the loss of someone or another. Across the street from the bar is Boettcher's Funeral Home, which is the very same funeral home that Walt happens to work at. Walt is the guy who arranges the orange flags that say Funeral on windshields of funeralgoers. He drives the hearse and leads the long funeral procession. He helps put the casket in the hearse and take it out, or if there are family members, he directs them how to do it. He has other duties as well, which he tells me about: he keeps the water bubblers full of water, for instance. He also talks business with the guys at all the local cemeteries—you know, the gravediggers and the folks who keep the chapels going. He also helps a bit, I'm told, consoling wild-eyed widows who stand near the water bubbler weeping uncontrollably into their cups. He's seen it all a thousand times. Since he's taken this job he's become curiously empathetic about the whole business, and at times he even tries to console me. Gideon, he says, placing a warm, soft hand gently on my clavicle and another around my bicep. You look like someone who's just buried the dead. Are you sure you're OK? Do you want to talk about it? I'm here for you if you need me.

Nevertheless, if I'm patient, the old Walt will invariably emerge. He'll have a few drinks, and the horrors of his past creep up on him, and all of a sudden it's too much. The dam breaks, the levee is overrun, and suddenly talking to Walt is like trying to talk to someone clinging to a tree before the floodwaters wash him away, and we revert to our old roles, with me as comforter and Walt as supplicant.

So when this guy in the suit pulls up his stool next to mine and says he was just at a funeral, I believe it.

Who'd you bury? I ask.

My mother.

Cheers, I say, tilting back the bottle.

He looked at me a bit oddly and took a sip from his bottle. Then I start telling him about that stupid book. Can you believe it, I say. I turn to Victor. Hey, Vic, how 'bout a couple of brandies here. This guy just buried his mom. I was slurring my words. Then I get back to the book.

When Vic puts the brandy glasses in front of us, the man in the suit demurs. No thanks. I want to remain clearheaded tonight. I'm only here a minute. Then I got to be off to the wake. My mother's laid out.

Well before you go, I say, have a drink.

So Vic pours us our brandy.

Cheers again, I say, throwing the brandy back. Now let me tell you something, I say. So I buttonhole this guy and tell him a thing or two about my uncle—how he's generous to a fault but how lately he's been putting pressure on me to put a life plan together. And I tell him my theory—how it's his wife, Nan, who's putting him up to it. That being said, my uncle wants me to put together a plan of my life with clear objectives—because, you see, he's been sending me monthly checks. So he wants a return on his money. And that's why he needs this plan. So when I'm not immediately forthcoming with this plan he—or rather his second wife, because, you see, his second wife is always putting him up to these kinds of things—sends me this book *What Color Is Your Parachute?* Have you heard of it? It's a lousy book.

But my new friend—the man in the suit—was not sympathetic. I'd like to pay up, he says to Victor, waving his fingers at him. How much for these? he says, pointing with two fingers to the brandies.

What do you mean, chrissakes? I tell him. This round's on me. Drink up. Geez, you just buried your mom!

No, really, he says. It's quite all right. Let me pay. Really, I should be going. Thank you very much.

So he pays up, and then, out of the blue, just before leaving, he says to me—I mean, this is his parting shot— By the way, I have a copy of that parachute book, and it helped me out of a jam ten years ago. It helped me realize that my two interests, animals and optometry, could be combined into a single career: animal optometry. I then developed a step-by-step plan with goals and outcomes that I followed very carefully—and that I learned how to do by reading that parachute book that you so disparage. As a result of that book, I was able to focus my way through veterinary school, and this I followed up with a residency in animal optometry. In ten years I went from dreaming about a career to owning my own animal eye clinic—and I have the parachute book to thank for it! With that, he set his brandy down on the bar. He thanked me; then he turned and thanked Victor. He was polite and civil as hell, and then he was gone. Gone with the wind to bury the dead, and I never saw him again.

ACTUALLY, AND I TOLD this story to Victor after the guy who buried his mother left, it occurred to me, sitting there, talking to this guy in the suit, that part of my problem—that is if you want to construe it as a problem—is I probably do need a parachute of some sort or another, only I'm too fond of the idea of free-falling. I was talking off my head that night, but there was a kernel of truth in what I said: I want to see how long I can go on my uncle's dough. Let the rest of the world work itself to death, but such is not for me. I like the idea of free-falling. Living on the edge. What's more, and this is a true fact, I've always wanted to leap from a plane fifteen thousand feet high and fall as long as possible while the earth, a patchwork of farms below, comes rushing toward me. Holding out on my uncle is a little like that, don't you think?

While I told all of this to Victor, he pointed out to me that I was still young and that I probably didn't know any better. This was Victor's opportunity to tell me that living off my uncle's money was not the same as living on the edge, but he remained mute on this issue, careful not to wound my sense of myself. In any event, Victor himself had spent World War II jumping from C47s into enemy fire, and he wouldn't wish free-falling without a parachute (literal or otherwise) on anyone. Last time I jumped from a plane it was in a field in Normandy. My chute closed up on me forty feet aboveground. When I crashed onto terra firma I made a promise to God: I said, if you get me through this I promise never to leave earth again. That's when I was shot. I left the war on a boat bound for home, and true to my word, I've never flown or jumped from a plane again, and if you had any sense you wouldn't do it either.

ALL OF THIS REMINDS ME of a guy I knew. We called him High-rise Harry because he was a skydiver. Jumping changed him fundamentally. Before his first jump, he was Harry to all of us who knew him, but after his first jump he was High-rise Harry. He was one of those lucky souls who found his true calling—skydiving—and he pursued it, once he discovered it, with monomaniacal zeal. He jumped from all sorts of planes and became interested in high altitude diving, which required special suits and oxygen canisters strapped to his chest. He told me leaping out of a plane was better than sex, and like a devoted husband he pursued it with monogamous fidelity. He said falling without a chute, no strings attached, was a dream of all skydivers—which is why he jumped higher and higher—to prolong the free fall. He said falling against the air was a little like lying on a bed made of wind. He would say you can try and imagine it, but the rush, the sheer bodily rush, is something you can never imagine.

MY FRIEND HIGH-RISE died one autumn day when his chute failed. He landed in the dirt in a field near Dixon, Illinois. Witnesses say an M-80 exploded nearby. When they turned they saw High-rise Harry's body buried in the turf.

WHEN I LEFT THE BAR that night—so drunk I could barely stand—Victor pulled me aside and said, Hey, kid, look: I don't like the direction you're headed. The world's your oyster: it beckons. You should be excited about that. Excited! Don't spend all your time hiding from it in this lousy dive. Use your uncle's money. Buy a suit. Then go out there and get a job!

I RESPECT VICTOR for his advice. To have the courage to give advice . . . I admire that. I've never been so inclined. What's more, my life is too messy and filled with mistakes to make me any sort of expert. Normally I would have spit in the eye of anyone trying to tell me how to live my life. But Victor was a special case. He loved me like a son and vice versa. He's the only reason why I kept drinking at the bar. You're my soul friend, I liked to tell him time to time, especially while he was pouring me brandy. No. Correction, he would say. *This is your sole friend.* Then we'd lift our glasses—cheers or *prost* or *nostrovia*— and down the hatch.

The world's your oyster, he said again, setting his glass down on the bar. It beckons.

It beckons? I asked him. How so?

You know what I mean, son. Don't waste all your time in here. Go home. Clean yourself up. Find a good job. Something that will make you happy. I know you don't need to work, but a job will do you good.

I still felt like asking Victor how a job would be good for me, but I drank my brandy down and kept my trap shut.

I went home that night, and in the mail was my monthly letter and a check from my uncle.

I FELL ASLEEP THINKING of what Victor had told me about the world beckoning. I tried to imagine him jumping from that C47 transport plane into that dark field and being shot to pieces. I was curious how he ended up here in Chicago running a bar. I promised myself that I would ask him one day. I tossed and turned the whole night and awoke in the morning with a hangover.

Instead of buying a suit, as I felt pressured to do, I bought a car instead. A car would be the beginning of a solution, I thought, to solving my problems.

There was a used car lot on South Western Avenue with signs out front that cryptically read: ABC123CARS CARS CARS!!! A 30-foot inflatable dinosaur was tethered by chain out in front of the dealership. I went down there, looked around a bit, and after much musing and kicking of gravel, I bought an '81 Chevy Chevette with 5-speed manual transmission for seven hundred bucks. If my uncle only knew how I was spending his money, I think he'd die automatically of a heart attack. My uncle is fond of driving around town in a Cadillac with all the features (heated seats, V8 engine, etc.) and is disdainful of spending money on garbage. More than once while visiting I heard him say: The problem with a used car . . .

Is there a problem, Uncle?

The problem with a used car, and there are many, is that they usually belong where you found them—in the junkyard.

Unlike my uncle or my brothers and father, I didn't yearn for cars. What kind of vehicle a person drives has never been of interest to me, and so, I've always been rather practical about how and in what sort of vehicle I should travel. My old Chevy Chevette is a perfect car for me. It's cheap. It gets me from here to there, which is really all that matters, right? Granted, it loses power on hills, but here in the Midwest—in Chicago, for goodness sake—where you don't see a hill until you hit Appalachia or the Rockies, who needs power? What's more, it has good air conditioning, heat, an AM/FM radio that reliably finds all the stations it needs to find on the lower end of the dial, and, most of all, the parts needed to repair it are still available and cheap at the local junkyard. What's more, it doesn't have any of these computer systems, which requires a master mechanic. So I, with the occasional help of my friend Walt, am able to do the repair work myself. He thinks the car is a piece of shit himself, but he likes working on it, and occasionally he even commends me for buying such a simple, useful car.

Not a bad car.

No not at all. But I don't care about cars anyway.

Suit yourself, but you could have done worse than this.

WALT, AS I MENTIONED, is a sort of all-purpose man at Boettcher's Funeral Home. Before joining up with the funeral business Walt was a crack mechanic for the Chicago and North Western Railroad. He repaired all those huge diesel electric engines on the locomotives. I'm told he was quite a mechanical genius. There wasn't a train he couldn't repair. One day his hand got all mangled when the spring on a coupler backfired, and he lost three fingers. After a long legal battle he received compensation for his injury, and when the opportunity presented itself for him to return to the railroad, he said to hell with it. He needed to take some time off. Recuperate. He'd been working at the railroad nonstop since he'd returned from the Vietnam War, and he wasn't getting any younger.

Should I die tomorrow, he told me (he was forty-eight at the time), what good would retirement at sixty-five do me? The time to retire is now. While I'm still young. While I still have my health, knock wood.

So that's what he did. He retired from the railroad and lived a year off his medical compensation. He had two hundred grand. A veritable gold mine, but he managed to spend it all until he was broke.

I discovered, rather quickly, that Walt was a gambling nut. He loved the horses. Since I didn't have a job and also, since, like Walt, I loved the horses, he and I would go out to the tracks (drive out there in my Chevette) and watch the horses run all day. I never bet more than ten bucks on a race; I had my limits. If I'm going to do this thing, I thought—live off my uncle's money—then I'm going to be frugal about it, at least while I'm here at the racetrack. Occasionally temptation would get the better of me, especially when I knew it was a sure thing, and then, with shaky hands, I'd splurge and lay all my money down. I always—and it's uncannily the case—lost those damned bets.

Walt was not nearly as frugal as me. He was a millionaire by my standards and acted like it. Over time he developed a foolish system—what he called, for some reason, "the metric system"—and it was based on a series of complicated algorithms that all pointed to the slowest, most lame horse in the field. It was a system that defied common sense, and when I pointed this out to him— when I told him that those nags were long shots because they were dud horses—he pointed out to me that the fact that it defied common sense was what recommended it as a good strategy, and what's more, occasionally a dud horse in the back of the field found game rounding the bend. It's true, he said, defiantly. They can win once! He thought he could short-circuit the science of horse betting—it was a science, wasn't it?—with his silly formula. His downfall was that he won big on that first long shot.

Of course after he devised the method behind his incomprehensible metric system, he made me promise never to divulge it. He looked at me and honored me by solemnly saying, Blood brothers don't betray. Needless to say, I was impressed that a man twice my age, and after all he had seen and done—hell he'd been sucked into the bloody fulcrum of a useless war and lived to tell about it—would take someone like me—a sponge soaking up my uncle's money—into his confidence.

Occasionally, Walt's system worked. Once in a while a horse with thirty-five to one odds would hit, and he'd be rolling, unexpectedly, in the dough. Those were glorious, glamorous days—and as you know there's no money quite like the money earned gambling. When he hit big we'd binge drink at all of our favorite bars downtown; we'd hire cabs and drive off to our favorite restaurants and eat like kings—all the seafood and steak we could consume at places like Cy's Crab House or Morton's The Steakhouse. Walt preferred lobster and top sirloin. I, on the other hand, craved Alaskan crab legs and prime rib. Eat, eat up! he would say. Please, it's all on me. He was the sort who got genuine pleasure out of seeing me stuff my face. My uncle's stipend didn't allow for me to pursue gluttony, but Walt's two-hundred thousand medical compensation and early victories at the racetrack did. After dining like kings we were off to, of all places, the opera. We'd get floor seats if we could, and once we even sat in the front row next to the conductor, getting spattered by his sweat while he waved his baton as if it were some sort of whip lashing the distant horn and percussion sections. Most of the time though, we were content to sit in the balcony hurling bravos mid-aria upon the singers as if they were curses. That's where people like us sat, and we felt comfortable peering through our binoculars—which weren't opera binoculars but binoculars designed for hunting game—at the cleavage of the women on the main floor and the beer-gut tenors who slew each other for their favors, and all the while we'd be beguiled by the triple echo of those glorious operatic voices that rose on the spires of air to touch us.

Though Walt was otherwise uncultured—he didn't read books or newspapers for instance and he couldn't care less whether a car came with an AM/FM radio, for he didn't listen to the radio—opera amounted to a great love. He had nostalgic ideas about opera, which he'd picked up from the movies. One of those ideas was that you should love it body and soul. Nicolas Cage, he of the wooden arm and love of opera in *Moonstruck*, had a great influence on him. Another nostalgic idea—he loved Wagner above all composers because, well, he'd fallen in love with opera during the helicopter scene of *Apocalypse Now*. He went out next morning, after that movie, and bought a tape of Wagner's greatest hits conducted by Eugene Ormandy: "Magic Fire Music" from *Die Walkure,* the Bridal Chorus from *Lohengrin,* "Forest Murmurs." This tape became the sound track to his life, and whenever he became maudlin, he would rummage around all the clutter in his one-bedroom apartment, find this tape under an old shoe, put it in the cassette player, and, together, we'd quietly sit in the lamplight of his kitchen, beer in hand, and contemplate our respective lives while Wagner and the Philadelphia Orchestra droned ravishingly on.

When we weren't going to the opera or the horse track, we loved going to all the comedy clubs on Wells Street in Old Town. We saw all the great Second City players in their heyday. We even saw John Belushi and Dan Aykroyd in their Blues Brothers routine just before Belushi perished in a hotel room on Sunset Boulevard from that speedball—and whenever his name comes up, which it does with increasing infrequency, I always like to point out that I was one of the last guys to see him perform live, and he was great! In fact, later the same night we saw them perform. Walt and I were walking through the alley just west of Wells Street, and there Belushi was, doubled over, vomiting into a bush. When he was done, he lifted his head and looked at us; his eyes were bloodshot and moving back and forth, scanning us, but a moment later he merely smiled and waved it all away.

Walt loved more than anything the stand-up routine, and just about anything would set him laughing uncontrollably, but I was a fan of the quick improv skit, and I never got over my fascination of how they did it, particularly if the thought of the improv was moving faster than what seemed possible. There were nights I would look over at Walt—he would look at me, and the two of us would start laughing so hard, I thought blood was going to start squirting out our eyes. As it was, more than once beer came out our noses, and the happiness from the laughter, well—there's nothing like it.

We always kept a lookout for females, but we never lucked out. Occasionally, after the comedy clubs shut, we'd drift down to Division Street, slip down the stairs to some subterranean basement with a disco ball, and we'd alternate between watching the bodies shake as we stood on the margins drinking or jumping right in—wading to the middle of the dance floor, shaking and jigging for all we were worth, which, judging from the results of our efforts, wasn't much. Somehow we'd end up at a 4:00 a.m. joint in search of liquor and an even more vain search for women, and by that point who knows how much we had drunk and what? A mélange of drinks: watermelon shots, Long Island iced teas, kamikazes, brewskis, shots of all stripes, coffee to keep us going, and a margarita or two just to get our salt intake to properly balanced levels. At the end of the night we had achieved that transcendental state brought on by fatigue and alcohol, and there were no worries because neither of us had to work the next day. We'd stumble back onto Division Street, which had been depopulated but for a few other drunken stragglers, and hail a cab. Off we'd go toward home; the cab would merge onto the expressway, the city and its wondrous architecture would rise up in the shadows of early morning, and there on the rim of the horizon just over the other side of the lake you could see the first lavender sprays of the dawn sun illuminate the bottom tufts and ripples of the overhanging cloud cover.

WALT HAD BEEN MARRIED once, long ago, before I ever knew him. He wasn't very forthcoming about the details of his brief marriage, and so for the larger part of our friendship, his marriage hung in his past—not like a historical incident but as a powerful legend steeped in myth and succored time to time by a sort of raw sexual nostalgia that would emerge particularly when he was drunk in the wee hours of the morning. Occasionally, he would tell me brief anecdotes about his former wife, whose name, I gathered, was Bonnie.

Piecing the anecdotes together, I've been able to surmise the following. When he returned from Vietnam, he was almost immediately married to a childhood sweetheart, Bonnie, but the marriage went south when, a year into it, he'd discovered her in the sack with a man, who, he recognized, was their regular postal carrier. The whole disaster of that experience—catching his naked wife in an amorous clutch with another man— was often relived in those late night drinking binges, and I will say this about Walt—which I think is quite notable—he never held anything against that man but placed the blame on his wife and some of it on himself. I knew we shouldn't have gotten married the moment I saw her coming down the aisle. I still had too much baggage from the war, and she couldn't understand that. My marriage didn't even last a year. Who knows how long she'd been fucking other guys.

Nevertheless, Walt also told me that when he came home that day and encountered that man penetrating his wife, a blind choking rage over came him. He tore the man off his wife and began beating him, smashing his head against the floor while his wife—naked, screaming— pulled at his shoulders and neck trying to get him to stop. You monster! You monster! Stop! When he finally did stop beating the man he went to his closet, pulled out a nickel-plated .38 (which he still keeps in his current bedroom closet—he shows it to me time to time), and he held it not to the man's forehead but to his wife's. Tell me why I shouldn't do this, he said. Give me one good reason. She was naked, on her knees; her hands were plaintively folded, pleading. He told me, how, holding the gun to his wife's forehead, he wished more than anything to pull the trigger. When she refused to answer

him (because as he later said, there was no good reason he shouldn't kill her and we both knew it) he had
a change of heart. He turned, stepped out of the door
and out of her life, and he never looked back. He let her
do her thing, he does his thing, and there's never any
interference. He occasionally sees her even now—for
she lives in town—driving around in a huge SUV. She
married a doctor and has three high school boys. He
occasionally still sees that mailman too. Once when we
were out drinking Walt noticed his former rival sitting
at the bar by himself watching NASCAR racing on the
tube. That's him, Walt pointed out. He's the one I almost
killed. Later that night when we left the bar—it was past
2:00 a.m.—Walt told me to wait for him by the door. I
stood near the entrance watching Walt. The jukebox was
playing "I Fall to Pieces" by Patsy Cline. There was a lot
of smoke; the place was dark and crowded. I watched
Walt tap the postal carrier on the shoulder and buy him
a drink. Upon seeing Walt, the postal carrier nearly ran
out the back door, but Walt grabbed hold of him and
held him in this big forgiving embrace. I mean Walt is
this square, solidly built man, and he grabbed this skin-
ny guy; he took him in his arms, and he gave him a bear
hug and a kiss on the cheek and he asked forgiveness.
Then they sat down and had a drink. They were talking.
I heard booming laughter. Then Walt got up, shook his
hand, and turned away, smiling. When he returned to
me, waiting for him at the door, his face was radiant as
he said, I apologized and he accepted. He told me bygones are bygones. I've a clean slate!

   After he and his wife parted ways, Walt moved into
this one-bedroom above mine. This is when we began

our year of cavorting, which came to an end when, after working in the funeral home a few months, he met this woman, Alice Macintyre, whom he lives with now. He met her at Oak Woods Cemetery after she lost her husband. Walt often saw her in the cemetery sobbing over her husband's tombstone. It was more than Walt could handle, seeing her cry like that. First he befriended her by asking about her husband, and then he told her bits and pieces of the story of his ruined relationship with Bonnie and the whole nightmare of fighting in Vietnam. They started dating, and within weeks of meeting each other they moved in together—she into his one-bedroom flat. I'll never forget the day Walt told me with a touch of triumph in his voice that he had a girlfriend. He told me how he met her, and then he said, She fell in love with my grief!

But what about you? What about you? I asked.

What about me, he said, a look of anger coming over his face. So I just dropped it. Not long thereafter we went our separate ways.

THE HORSES RUINED Walt's early retirement. I felt somewhat to blame. We'd developed a habit of driving out to Sportsman's Park, spending irresponsible days gambling, spending incredible amounts of his retirement cash, getting drunk on the proceeds on the rare occasions we won—and even on many of the occasions we lost. And some days when I invited him to join me at the park and he was reluctant to come, I used what influence I had over Walt to make him come along anyway.

Come on. It's a beautiful day. You don't want to sit inside all day, do you?

I'm hungover and I'm broke. I'm above the number I said I would spend on horses for this month. You'll have to go it alone.

I can't go without you. What would be the fun in that? You're my good luck charm. I promise, if you come, we'll leave by the seventh race.

And so Walt would reluctantly agree to come along, and once there he'd lose his senses and bet inordinate sums on long shots. We'd get drunk too, which impaired his judgment. Suddenly money wasn't this thing that plugged into the economy but a ticket to continue playing the horses, and playing the horses became a ticket to losing money, and losing money became a reason to bet ever larger sums to recover what had been lost so that we could carry on and continue to play. It was a vicious cycle. In this way, Walt had run out of all his money by the end of the year—one hundred thousand dollars of it or so—and he was forced, at the ripe age of forty-nine, after exactly one year of retirement, to rejoin the workforce.

I remember when he told me he was broke. We'd been sitting around the table. We were listening to Wagner's *Lohengrin*. It was late at night. The conversation between us, intermittent though it was, had been unsatisfying. Walt had seemed cagey. After several hours of this I grew pissed off and got up to leave.

I've got better things to do than sit here with you!

Just then he attempted to apologize to me.

Apologize for what? I asked. Wagner was blasting in the background. I swear, sometimes I thought Walt was deaf.

I'm broke. I've got to go back to work. Our days at the races are through. I'm sorry.

Inexplicably, I started to laugh. Of course there was nothing to laugh at, but once I got going I couldn't stop. It was, for some reason, the funniest thing I'd ever heard—funnier than all of the combined jokes of all the stand-up routines we had ever seen. Of course it was a tragedy that Walt lost such a large sum of money, and I was a fool for laughing at him for doing so. But I couldn't help myself. I don't know why. Maybe it was the time of night and the Wagner music rumbling like thunder. And I must admit, I've never liked Wagner, and Walt's rapture with this sort of thing is precisely what irritated me about him. Anyway there was the music, his confession, my laughter. Maybe it was the way Walt told me, all hangdog and apologetic. Maybe it's because it scared the hell out of me—for it was me, after all, who had contributed to his demise. It was me who had ruined him by taking him to the tracks day in, day out. When he was spiraling down a vortex of loss and losing and mounting long shots that didn't pan out, I merely stood by, fascinated by the tragic splendor of it, and I did nothing to stop him. In fact, I egged him on. Go ahead: double your bet. If it hits we're good for the day and out of trouble for the week! I don't know why, but this suddenly seemed mad and hilarious all at once.

Walt was stunned by my performance. He looked at me as if I were a bit odd, and it struck me that it was just now occurring to him that his loss and my loss were not equal—that his was much greater, with deeper tragic resonance, and that I had come along to enjoy the show. Instead of apologizing for my behavior, I merely said good-night, stumbled down the stairs to my apartment, which was directly below his, and slammed the door behind me. I sat drinking alone in my apartment listening to Walt bang around above me—banging around until he or I collapsed from drink and fatigue—and what happened after that is lost from memory. What is not lost from memory is that within two years of that moment he was dead of an aggressive cancer to the lymph nodes brought on by exposure to Agent Orange.

IN THE MORNING when I awoke, I saw in the pile of advertising circulars a letter addressed to me in my uncle's telltale hand—a steady octogenarian hand, steadier than mine—that formed precise geometric letters angled slightly to the right, each letter proximal to the next so the whole line looked like a good set of teeth. I imagined a set of teeth in a gaping smile and behind that smile would hopefully be a check.

I opened the envelope. And there it was. A check fell out. I unfolded the letter and read.

> Dear Gideon,
>
>   Spent all day Monday and Tuesday at the doctors. All sorts of specialists trying to get at what's wrong with Nan. Her abdomen is in chronic pain, but thankfully, after C-Scan and MRI it was determined that CANCER is not the problem—thank god, knock wood—but that leaves open the question of what is the problem. Thursday liver specialist, and next week out to St. Petersburg to see famous Jewish endocrinologist by the name of Broch. In the meantime, got out on the boat this morning for a little snook fishing in the canals as it's middle of snook season. Caught three keepers

but let them go because Nan won't eat them. Also caught one thirty-pound grouper, which was also released. Sunburned my scalp when cap was lost yesterday in high wind. It blew into a water trap with three full-grown alligators and 8 holes of golf yet to finish. Hope this tides you over. Please note: a little bump in the number, as inflation is only getting worse. Have you thought of professional school while you put together your plan? Just a thought.

Love always,

Unc.

To which I responded:

Dear Uncle Eddie,

Everything is going superlatively well. I'm working on my plan. Did I mention how useful Nan's gift of the book *What Color Is Your Parachute?* was to me? It made me think of becoming a skydiver. Do extend to her my gratitude and my hopes to her for a speedy recovery.

Love from your nephew,

Gideon

I sealed the letter in an envelope and walked down the stairs to the sidewalk. It was noon and blazing hot. It took a moment for my eyes to adjust. After I deposited the note in the mailbox on the corner, I made a decision to spend the rest of the day in the cool shadows of the tavern, recovering from that crazy night with Walt and preparing myself for the week to come.

INITIALLY WALT WANTED to go back to work as a mechanic—
it was his métier after all—but with his three fingers
lopped off, finding work in a shop was probably slim.

One afternoon while drinking beer at our tavern, Walt
encountered the owner of Boettcher's Funeral Home
who had come in to slake his thirst with a beer. John
Boettcher was a tall, wire-thin man with deep-set eyes
and a large set of teeth that looked like they belonged
on some sort of furry herbivore. From the teeth, which
his lips seemed barely able to conceal, you could divine
the shape of his skull—a boney-hollow, long-jawed skull
with heavy ridges over the eyes. Who knows, maybe the
Cro-Magnon line wasn't finished after all. What's more,
John Boettcher always wore black. If he wasn't the grim
reaper, he certainly was a good stand-in, and I'm sure
children never trick-or-treated his house for fear that he
was the real thing. That night when he stopped in at Sal's
for a beer, he told us he was desperate for help. He'd just
lost two of his people: they fled to Mexico when immi-
gration officials came around. As a result, he was now
forced to hire aboveboard, and he needed a couple of assistants fast. The jobs he was offering paid $28,000 a year
with benefits plus 2% of the profits. It included overtime
and holiday pay, and he promised that if we stayed in the
business with him long enough that it was conceivable—
that, the funeral business being what it was, which was in
a state of consolidation—we could be making upward of
$60,000 per annum within a few years. The deal sounded
too good to be true—one minute illegal immigrants, the
next minute us?—and the man making the pitch, Mr.
Boettcher, seemed too slick to be believable. He had a
reputation in town for being a tightwad. There was a

saying among the people in the neighborhood: When I die—whatever you do—don't send me to Boettcher's. Yet everyone, sooner or later, whether they willed it or not, ended up under Boettcher's knife while he prepared the body for embalmment and by hook or crook—depending on how one lived life—for the afterlife.

I had made a vow with myself not to work until I found something that was appropriate for me. What's appropriate? Well I was pretty certain preparing corpses wasn't it. What's more, I worried what my uncle would say when I told him that I had begun a career in the funeral business. You haven't come this far in life only to become a gravedigger, have you? No, I could never take John Boettcher's offer seriously—not to mention, I could never take him seriously, what with his ghoulish looks and ghoulish business. I'd rather drink and die than sign up with him. Such was my conviction at the time.

WALT WAS A DIFFERENT STORY altogether. He didn't quite have the same sense of himself that I had of myself. A job was a job to him, and he was never too good to stoop and take it, especially now that he needed the loot. Hell, I've been a soldier in the Vietnam War, he'd remind me time to time. It doesn't get lower than that. What's more, due to his now diminished resources, he was considerably more desperate to work than I was. Boettcher's pitch was too much for Walt to resist. He liked the idea of earning in excess of sixty grand at some point within the next few years, and so, a beer and a handshake later, he joined on to work for John Boettcher at the funeral home.

You sure you don't want to join me, buddy? Walt asked. This could be your opportunity—our opportunity—

working together. Who knows, maybe one day we can go into business by ourselves.

Not right now, I said. Maybe later.

There's always an opportunity to earn money part time in this business, Boettcher chimed in. As they say, people are dying for my services. He chuckled at his own stale graveyard humor and gave me his card. I know who you are. You strike me as good people. Call anytime you want if you need a little extra dough.

AFTER WALT MET ALICE, which was, as I said, not long after he took a job at Boettcher's, we quietly began to drift apart. It was more my doing than his. What's more, it seemed only natural that we should go our separate ways. Our friendship was based upon a.) proximity to each other (he lived in the flat directly above mine) and b.) availability. Since we were both single and since neither of us had a job for the time Walt was temporarily "retired," ours was the perfect friendship. But with his job and then with his girlfriend, with whom I had nothing in common, it was only natural that we drifted apart. I suppose I'm the one who can be blamed for the demise of the whole friendship between Walt and me. He made several overtures to me; I rebuffed him. I didn't like his girlfriend, and what's worse, I didn't like Walt under the influence of his girlfriend.

Let's get a drink, he would say whenever she was working the late shift.

Sorry, I would tell Walt, knowing I was breaking his heart. I'm awfully busy.

Like hell, he would say. Let's go down to the track or something.

Wish I could, I would tell him. But tonight's not a good night.

Well, Alice doesn't work next week. Perhaps next Tuesday we can get together.

We'll see what happens next Tuesday. For the time being I don't like to plan that far ahead. Never know what may come up.

And so it went.

I'd pull a chair into the middle of my room, and with a glass pressed to the ceiling and my ear pressed to the glass, I'd spend long evenings eavesdropping on Walt and his new girlfriend. It seemed they talked about anything and everything under the sun, and just when I thought my own name should come up in conversation, it never did.

4:00 a.m.

I wake myself to write. I should be sleeping like the rest of the world, but I'm wide awake on my couch, drinking a can of Bud and watching the everlasting tube. If I were a dog, I'd be a mongrel mutt. I feel homeless, shiftless. It's 4:00 a.m. I want to howl at the moon. Actually, I'm not watching so much as gazing at the bright screen. I'm gazing at it for a lack of anything better to gaze at. Had it been a different era, pre-TV, pre-electricity, I might just as well have hung an oil lamp and watched the flame flicker, the wick slowly disappearing to ash. Instead, I'm sitting on my black vinyl couch, which is actually a pull-out bed—and there was a time when I used to pull the couch open into a bed, but anymore, I just grab a hand-knit afghan from the closet and curl up on the couch, gaze at the tube, and let it lull me to sleep. But tonight when I get the call, I'm half-drunk, having passed the last several hours at the bar where my girlfriend—the one who told me I was the love of her life, the one who speculated that she and I would be married—and I had words that approached an ultimatum. In fact, I just hung up the phone with Claire. She's angry to the point of incoherence. She screamed into the phone, and I turned it away toward the room to soften the blow of her screaming voice. She was saying things she shouldn't have said. She called me a loser. She said she couldn't believe that someone with my gifts—your *gifts!* she said—is squandering it all drinking beer at that lousy tavern down the street night after night. She said it again: I can't wait on you forever, Gideon. She intimated that it's embarrassing to be seen with such a sloth as me. And then she asked, Do you really want to know what my friends think?

No, but go ahead.

They think you're useless. They think I should dump you, and in truth I don't see why I shouldn't!

On and on she ranted. And then there was a moment of silence, and then: Gideon, I can't believe you're making me feel this kind of pain! I thought I heard a sob. Who knows, she might have just been taking a breath. The silence was prolonged, and, I sensed, I was being somewhat hurtful—a jackass more like it—because I felt she was awaiting a response from me. A significant response, but I had none. At the very least I should say some word to comfort her. I sensed she wanted a small kind word, but I withheld my consolation. Go ahead, suffer, I thought. You get what you deserve. Of course I didn't have the courage to say this. I only had courage enough to be silent. Suddenly she said, I need to know tomorrow, Gideon, whether you're coming with me or not to New York City. With that, she hung up the phone.

And now I'm awake. Besides the beer, I'm also suffering from indigestion, which is, I suppose, due to nerves, but it's also due to all the crap I've been eating. And I've been eating a lot of crap in search of, I suppose, comfort. Earlier in the evening, for instance, before meeting Claire at the tavern, I walked past a KFC, and not being able to resist, I went in and ordered a bucket of extra crispy chicken and ate the whole thing myself. And then, at the bar, with Claire by my side, I ordered a double

cheeseburger and a large order of fries. I also drank several pitchers of beer to wash it down while Claire sulked
and nursed hers.

It worries me, frankly, all this spending on crap food
and beer because this unbridled spending is a luxury I
feel I can no longer afford. And that's part of the reason
why I'm up at 4:00 a.m. watching first Charles Rose on
CBS News's *Nightwatch* interview some celebrity or another and then an old ineffective Western with old ineffective John Wayne. I've never liked John Wayne. I'm
prejudiced against him, always have been and I don't
know why. To my mind he's got one chief problem as
an actor: he doesn't believe in the characters he plays.
As a result, I've never been able to believe in him. Is
that a stupid thing to say? Maybe. However, watch and
you'll see. He comes across as graceful but insincere.
He's a big, bulky, hollow—graceful, yes—but hollow
man's man. I've had arguments with friends about this—
friendship-breaking arguments—wherein I've gone so
far as to declare John Wayne a disingenuous fraud. But
my friends—some of whom are probably too educated
for their own good—see him as a sort of secular saint in
the era of pop, whatever the hell that means. It doesn't,
however, discredit my argument that he's a disingenuous
fraud. What the hell's a secular saint anyway? I ask. But
I guess that's part of my problem: I'm unable to let the
superficial things just slide by.

Anyway my nerves are on edge partly because of
Claire, partly because of this damned money problem.
I'm terrified to be receiving handouts that could stop.
I'm terrified partly because it's not the sort of life I en-
visioned for myself, partly because before I've even had

a chance to begin I feel finished—washed up, at the end of my rope—and to think, I hope to live past the age of thirty. Actually at one time I harbored fantasies of living past the age of eighty. But that's before I picked up cigarette smoking—a two-pack-a-day habit—which, despite my best efforts, I've been unable to quit, and it was also before I started drinking, which I've also been unable to kick. I suppose I like alcohol more than I ought. In reality I probably like alcohol more dearly than anything else at this moment in time, which is perhaps a bit unseemly especially in one so young, and I suppose one day I'll look back at this time in my life and shake my head over what was lost due to all this damned drinking. I also like sleep quite a bit, and I spend long days in bed—no matter how wonderful the weather—not getting up to do a damned thing except shit and piss. Just lying there, indolent, whiling the hours away—as if I had an infinite supply of hours or, more to the point, as if I were cowering from the damned world. I wish I was one of those people you see time to time at parties: a teetotaler. It took me a year to figure out how to pronounce that word, but now I've got it under my belt. I used to make fun of teetotalers as if they were religious fanatics in an era bereft of god. But how I admire the hell out of them now. I admire their ability to say no, even under tremendous peer pressure, and drink Coke instead or water, and, what's more, they still seem to have a good time. They are, in my opinion, the true secular saints of this world, and I wish that I was one of them. I wish I could go to a party and have fun without getting tanked on beer. I wish I had the discipline to say no to my vices: No to sleep! Down, cigarettes! Get away, beer! So long, junk food! You're ruining my life. I admire people with discipline. I always have. In fact, it had once been a brief aspiration of mine to join the Marines in order to obtain discipline. I was in high school at the time, and in my particular high school everyone I knew seemed off to join the military for no other reason than to obtain discipline. But I rapidly realized that either you have discipline or you don't, and if you don't have it to begin with, well, heaven help you—especially if you've joined the Marines.

Actually I admire people who have so much going on in their lives that they don't have time for vices. I see people like this everywhere. Many people I know, for instance, are stuck in eighty-hour-a-week jobs. Advertising. Investment banking. Corporate law. Consultancy. I've heard stories that some of them sleep in their cubicles because it wastes precious time taking the long commute home and getting a proper night's sleep in bed. I see people—neighbors of mine—holding down not one but two jobs and raising a family to boot. When I see them in the hallway, they are either coming home from one job or going off to the other. When I ask them how they're holding up, always it's the same refrain: Busy as hell.

How do people know what they want out of life? So many people seem so sure of themselves, of their lives, of their direction. I knew a friend who met a woman and within moments declared: I'm going to marry you. That was three winters ago. I was there. I was standing by his side at a party. I thought he was drunk, but six months later in August he went on and did just that—he married her. I saw it firsthand. I was invited to the wedding.

I got drunk and made a fool of myself by trying to have too intimate a dance with the bride. She was a beautiful woman from the North Shore, with radiant eyes and a big head of gorgeous red hair, and I couldn't help myself. I held her close. I dropped my head down on her shoulder. I lowered my hands to her hips and pushed my pelvis close to hers. I thought of her naked while I held her there on the dance floor. I'd nearly seen her naked several times—always scantily clad in a bikini. Her old man was president of some bank. They had a lovely house in Winnetka with a pool. I was often invited that summer for barbeques, and now I was here, invited to her wedding and wishing it were me and not him who was marrying her. The thing I'll never forget is that she let me dance like that. She did not object. She could be sexy as hell, a flirt. She was a little drunk too. She rested her forehead against my chest. I thought I heard a gasp of pleasure. You look ravishing, I told her and immediately felt stupid. I wanted to tell her something else: that I loved her, but I didn't have the courage. What's more, I used that stupid word, "ravishing." What is ravishing? Ravishing is nothing compared to her. She was transcendent, and I told her so. You're more than ravishing, you're . . .

Thank you, Gideon, she said.

After a moment more in her intimate embrace, I couldn't contain myself. I said, I love you. Always have. From the moment I met you. I wish that you hadn't gone with him.

She lifted her beautiful head; her eyes were deep pools of dark water. She was a little drunk, and she kissed me on the cheek very close to my lips. It was lurid as hell. I thought I was going to pass out. I've loved you too, she said. But you never made a move. Never! Whereupon she pushed me off and walked off the dance floor.

That night was the last I ever saw of her or of my friend. Her father took my friend on in the firm, and they moved to New York City where he does mergers and acquisitions. I hear he works like hell and makes something in the low six figures. What's more, they remain married to this day, and that was nearly three years ago: a lifetime in marriage years! They have one-year-old twin girls to boot. How I wish she had been mine. And yet I know that we wouldn't have lasted three years. Hell, we might not have even survived the engagement before she started to hate me for my lack of ambition, my slothfulness. I can hear her screaming now: Where's your backbone? Don't you have any hopes or desires? And me replying, You're it! You're my high watermark. It's all downhill from here.

AND IT'S TRUE. I have no ambition. What comes easily for many people—constructing plans, goals, a life—has not come so easily for me. I don't know what I want out of this life. Truly. And I don't have any great plans or hopes or aspirations. If in thirty years I haven't advanced from where I am now, I could care less. If I don't live to be thirty years older than I am now, it wouldn't bother me. After all, what's the point of piling up all these years? I've lived. Better to have lived and make a quick exit—make room for somebody else. How much does one need, after all, before it all becomes so repetitive? Should I point out that most humans prior to the modern era hardly lived longer than the common ape? Thirty, forty years was old age. By that reckoning I'm already a middle-aged man closer to death than to birth. What's more, the whole concept of working on a treadmill only to end up old and broken with your legs chopped off from diabetes or with a breathing hole poked into your throat as a result of cancer or, heaven help you, losing your memory, your continence, sitting in diapers in front of the tube being pushed around by a nurse. I mean, what's the point? Titans of industry have slaved and earned millions only for this! Better to die young, I say.

Where's your oomph? someone once asked when they saw how I moped around my apartment or clung, barnaclelike, to the bar. I was sorely tempted to say: That's what I'd like to know! The oomph gene is something I was born without. Try though I might to construct a plan, nothing really comes to mind. Nothing.

I TELL THIS TO CLAIRE, but she doesn't believe me. I tell her I'm a compass without a magnet: all directions seem feasible, but none jumps out. When I told her, quite sincerely, that I don't expect to live past the age of thirty, she mocked me as if I were a fool.

That sounds like a little boy talking, she said. Those are the words of someone who doesn't know what the world portends. Someone who's very spoiled.

Perhaps.

Claire has been pushing for me to make a more serious move on her. She's been pushing since the day we met. She wants me to leave my comfortable life behind in Chicago and go to New York with her where she and I—like my friend and his ravishing redhead—can begin building a life together with kids, a home, jobs.

I can't leave, I tell her. I've got all this stuff I'm fond of. I like the place too.

You're kidding, Gideon. What's there to like? This place is squalid. Your life is squalid and sad.

I like the neighborhood, I tell her. I like my couch, my TV. I have friends.

This is a university community. You live next to an SRO for god's sake, she points out. People come and go all the time. You're junk isn't so precious, believe me. Leave it behind. We'll buy new stuff. What's more, there are plenty of interesting people in New York just waiting to be your friend. You'll see.

I'VE MENTIONED THIS to some of my friends at the bar— whom she views as so replaceable. I've mentioned it to Vic as well, the bartender—a man whom I turn to for important advice. He's eighty years old, a veteran of the Second World War, where, in the fields of Normandy, he distinguished himself by getting his left leg shot off. He limps with an artificial appendage and works like hell behind the bar. His handicap is neither here nor there; however, there's something about him—an extreme and fastidious reserve, a parsimony—that appeals to me. It's as if he knows, after all he's seen and participated in—after war and all the sad drunken tales he's suffered through as a bartender—that silence is the beginning of wisdom. When I told him that Claire wants me to follow her to NYC, he responded cryptically enough: Make sure you chose wisely, son.

My thoughts exactly! And that's what I like about Vic. Had I asked anyone else—anyone who has ever set eyes on Claire—they would have told me to pick up and move. My old roommate, Neal, is a case in point. I'll never forget his immortal words when I complained that she wanted me to commit: Are you crazy, Anderson? You've struck pay dirt! He was an inveterate social climber, and he couldn't believe my good fortune. You'll never find someone as beautiful or rich as she. What's wrong with you?

I shrugged my shoulders.

OK then, do yourself a favor. Go to New York. Marry her. Do whatever she tells you to do. And for god's sake, quit your complaining!

TONIGHT, IN THE TAVERN, in front of Vic and the others, Claire very publicly gave me her ultimatum. I'm leaving for New York, she said with more than a little finality and frustration. In two weeks I'll be gone. I've hired movers. You can bring your stuff along if you like. Now's your chance to decide. Do you want to come with me and do something with your life, or, with the help of your uncle's money, do you want to just disappear from the world in this hole the rest of your life?

I didn't like the way she put that so I said, I'll take my chances here.

Whereupon she asked in a voice louder than I would have liked: Is that it? Is that your answer?

Yes.

And even more loudly touched with defiance but also with a certain tenderness: You have two weeks to change your mind, Gideon. In the meantime, do me a favor: keep your distance.

And out the door she went with a bang.

AFTER SHE LEFT, the place seemed considerably emptier. Two guys were at the pool table, and a few others were lined up to play, otherwise I would have shot a game. Occasionally Vic gazed over at me with a mournful expression, wondering whether to say his three or four words or whether to leave well enough alone. He chose well enough alone and merely placed a brandy shot in front of me. I was happy as hell for the gesture—for the vote of confidence, especially in the face of the rest of the drunks, who would, I promise you, never forget that I'd just been made a fool of and therefore, I suppose, more than a few realized right then that I was no better than they. They saw that I too was a common bum, a lout—despite my uncle's money—scorned by women, with no bright future.

I sat there for several hours—thinking and drinking and thinking until I could drink or think no more. That's when I wished that Claire would just pick up and split without me. I try to say those words: Go ahead. Go without me. They're odd words, and I'm unpracticed at saying them, because until now it has never occurred to me that I might indeed have to say them. Go, Claire, go back home to New York where you belong. I will stay here where I belong. God bless you in your endeavors and god bless me in mine. May you do well; may you be happy, joyful, but for the sake of Christ leave me before I drag you down. I wish you no ill will and hope you shall find someone more attuned to your ambitions than I have been.

With that, I picked up and dragged myself home.

I SLEPT IMPERFECTLY, and then there was that call of hers, and after the call sleep came intermittently. I chronically suffer from terrible bouts of insomnia. Night after night, I suffer from an inability to sleep. I seem to have lost the trick to just close my eyes and sleep. I remember a time when nothing could prevent me from sleeping. And now there's this call of hers, which rattles me from the shallows of a gray slumber, and so with eyes open I lay and stare at the shadows and weigh the pros and cons of the situation.

A few details. Where to begin? First of all—how we met. We met at a coffee shop, but let me tell you what happened a little before that. It was an utterly perfect day. I was still a student at the university. I remember it well. In fact, I was sitting in the quad reading J.D. Salinger's *Nine Stories.* I'd just closed the book after having read "A Perfect Day for Bananafish." What can I say? I was feeling sentimental. Spring gripped hold of me and nearly tipped me over, full of joy. A late afternoon light, peculiar, perhaps, to May evenings in Chicago, illuminated the newly budding leaves on the trees. There I was alone—for I was always alone back then (I retain romantic notions of loneliness), and I'm reading the tragic story of a World War II vet who entertains a little girl and then blows his brains out. I closed the book and felt not sadness but an epiphany totally unrelated to the experience of reading the story—an epiphany the exact nature of which I cannot explain. I felt rejuvenated from a cold dark Chicago winter, as if the spring air had just purified my blood. I felt renewed from the dark winter months in which I had labored away at writing essays and reading thick tomes such as *The Wealth of Nations.* More frequently, I avoided my studies altogether and spent long hours in taverns with various cronies getting as drunk as our pecuniary situations would allow and, often, getting sick enough next morning to render me homebound and ineffectual to do anything other than smoke cigarettes and watch TV. That spring afternoon in the quad, I don't recall if I was hungover or not, but I do remember having an indelible remembrance of my maternal grandmother, Nancy—a portly woman, barely five feet tall, of Eastern European peasant stock. She'd been widowed when my grandfather, Barney, a truckdriver, flipped his truck on the expressway to avoid hitting a drunken hitchhiker who had wandered into his lane of traffic for a ride. His truck flipped, went up in flames. To the hitchhiker's credit, he pulled my grandfather from the burning wreck. And then something remarkable happened: my grandfather was airlifted by helicopter to a local hospital where he died a week later of burns over 70 percent of his body. But he was one of the first people ever to be helicoptered to a hospital. As a result, there are newspaper reports of his mishap recorded in all of the local papers of the day, as well as a mention of the new rescue technology in *The New York Times*. I have clips of the articles, and I keep them in a manila file along with other things of his: photos, letters—between him and my grandmother—and an old catechism book that he had studied in a parochial school. Scattered throughout the book are his doodles: crude stick-figure renderings of naked girls with surprisingly voluptuous breasts that remind me somehow of ancient fertility figures—and this he did when he was seven or eight years old in 1918, the year of the great influenza, which, incidentally, my grandfather had caught and nearly succumbed to, but he survived. This makes me wonder about the margin of error that keeps us here. Had he died that winter by influenza—instead of by those terrible burns four decades later—I would not have been here, but he hung on, and the rest is history.

I lay down in the grass, J.D. Salinger clutched to my breast, when I suddenly remembered Nancy, my grandmother, with such keen vividness—such pungency—it was as if she'd instantly emerged from the ether of the netherworld or purgatory or wherever it is spirits reside—emerged to spend a few moments of the afternoon on the lawn with me. She was wearing a white cotton dress, which was none too graceful on her stout body, and she was considerably younger than I remembered her. In fact, I'd never known my grandmother but as a grandmother—never as a desirable young woman who had sexual desires of her own or the looks to appeal to my grandfather, the artist of those fertility symbols. When I entered the world she was as grandmotherly as could be at seventy-six years of age, and as such she was very generous and affectionate to me. She was the one person in the world I loved without qualifications. Our relationship was simple, easy; there were no complications between us. I felt she knew me through and through. As a result we had many open, candid, and wonderful conversations. She loved birds, for instance, and gardens. She talked often of her husband who had died before I was born. Together we spent many pleasant hours. But she died suddenly of an aneurysm. She was standing on a curb, waiting for a city bus, when she collapsed. I remember receiving the news hours later and being struck with a grief I'd never before experienced. At the funeral I'd said a little speech, then helped bury her by shoveling clods of dirt onto her casket. And then, soon after, I went back to living my life and nearly forgot all about her.

That afternoon out in the quad, she sat down next to me beneath a hickory tree. I felt the old warmth, the same candidness. She sat only for a moment, but before she left, she touched me and told me that her life—despite its many disappointments—had been happy and full of love. She was glad she had lived it. After she left I sat a moment more out on the lawn. I was acutely aware of the grackles and sparrows and crows in the treetops, the fresh spring breeze had the odor of flowers, and green grass and the people walking through the quad looked beautiful, and I fell in love with all of humanity. Such was my epiphany.

AFTERWARD I SHOOK it all off and walked over to the campus coffee shop for a coffee and a smoke.

I needed a pack of cigarettes for I was starting to get the jitters. When I walked into the smoky little shop crammed with a bunch of students, there she was, Claire, sitting alone, reading a book. She lifted her head from the page when she saw me, and on a whim, I walked over and asked if I could sit down. Claire is a lovely girl, striking really, a beauty. That afternoon in the coffee shop, she seemed beyond me. Yet I was hungover from my epiphany and filled with a sort of calm and peacefulness. What seemed formerly complicated was suddenly no longer the case—for I was usually always either too excitable or too depressed or too nervous or too lethargic or too foggy-headed or too light-headed or too clearheaded, or sometimes I feel like I'm itching all over. Other times I feel like I want to vomit with anxiety, and yet other times I feel so self-conscious that I can barely walk across a room—and always I'm drinking coffee or smoking cigarettes or drinking alcohol or sleeping or exercising or taking headache medicine to try to establish what that afternoon, after my grandmother's visitation, had come naturally to me: calm.

Please, she said, sit down. She looked and smiled on me as if somehow or other I might rise to the occasion of her beauty and take her. She was somewhat reserved at first, which surprised yet pleased me—for up until then all the women I had dated (all four of them) were either aggressively loud or shyly timid. I never seemed able to get the pitch right, but with Claire I felt on the cusp of a revelation—as if I'd been shown into the back room of an art gallery where paintings of astonishing beauty were suddenly available to me in my price range. My life, which seemed, up until that point, difficult and chaotic, suddenly felt easy, as if it had resolved into a harmonic chord. The elegance of her reserve was rare. It made me think at once that she was royalty, or could be, in a different era. And if only I attached myself to her, who knows, but perhaps that would elevate me as well. A stupid thought, really. And, retrospectively, I feel stupid for having had it. Later, when we were in bed, I would call her my queen or my princess and she would tap her naked toe on my nose and rub her bare calf along my cheek and say, Shut up, and adore me without words.

Sitting down across from Claire at the coffee shop, I made some trivial observation, which made her laugh. Her laughter was light, skittish, buoyant, and she was lovely while she laughed. There was a moment's pause, and then she said something to me that was really very funny, and I started laughing—and while I laughed I felt something strange happen: I felt as if I were shaking off the melancholy of a lifetime. A second later she was touching my feet with hers, and that's all there was to it. Our love affair had begun. We left the coffee shop as soon as we finished our drinks and stepped into a beautiful spring evening, which smelled of tar, lilacs, and diesel smoke from a passing truck. I was still in love with humanity, and I told her so.

And what about her? she asked, pointing to a student loaded down with books. She wore a black trench coat and heavy boots. Do you love her?

Would it make you jealous if I said so?

Yes.

Then I don't love her. Nor do I relish people in the particular, only en masse. I love humanity in an operatic sort of way.

In a Puccini way or a Verdi way?

A Puccini way, I said. In his *Madame Butterfly* phase.

Well I love humanity in a Verdi *Requiem* way. I love it fiercely, passionately!

Morbidly.

Not at all. Verdi wasn't morbid. *The Requiem* is fierce, passionate—but not morbid. Apropos of nothing, she grabbed my hand. I hope you don't mind me saying this, but I think I love you too. You as a specific, particular, unique human.

Do you always make such snap judgments?

Always. You'll see. I'm legendary for them.

I liked the way she said legendary. It was cute and entirely in keeping with her personality; she was as candid and electrifying as I imagined any Hollywood legend might be. She stopped abruptly on the sidewalk and kissed me flush on the lips.

That's another one of my snap judgments. I hope you agree with it.

I do. And, please, make them as often as you wish. We laughed when I said this.

It's strange to say, but even though it was me who approached Claire in the coffee shop, nevertheless it was she who chose me. She chose me so quickly and forthrightly that I didn't have a chance to decide whether I wanted to be chosen by her. Be careful for what you wish, an old saying goes, because you might get it! Later, when curious friends asked how our relationship began (which, by the way, was so unusual to them—everybody always used to say we were an odd couple: she an extrovert, me a curmudgeon), the standard story we gave was that I stepped into the coffee shop one early spring afternoon and picked her out of a crowd. How we shape the past according to our desires and wash over the truth! She picked me: that's the definitive truth, yet as the months of our relationship progressed, the truth slowly got buried beneath the legend of me selecting her—as if I were plucking the first flower of spring.

We headed over to a local Thai restaurant, which was very crowded. She saw friends of hers, grabbed my hand, and we walked over and sat down with them.

NOW I'LL ATTEMPT to recreate the dialogue. It went something like this:

Hi, everybody. This is Gideon.

There were four girls, each of whom gave me and then Claire an approving look. Claire took my hand and introduced me to everyone. Gideon, this is Marisa. She's from Bogota, Columbia. She's studying ancient Greek and is going to Harvard for grad school next year. This is Regina. She went to Dalton with me. She's majoring in economics and has a job with Merrill Lynch, but in reality she's a painter with a studio on the other side of the Midway. This is Maya—she comes to us from Iran—and studies the history of religion and wants to be a professor. And this is Molly, born and raised right here in Chicago. She's studying art history and wants to be an architect.

Hi, I'm Gideon. I study people, and I want to eat.

You mean psychology? Regina asked.

No, I mean people. I study people like you, whom I meet.

Oh, so sociology.

No, people.

So what's your major?

Oh, my major is English. But that doesn't really matter.

Why doesn't it matter?

I'm sorry, it does matter.

What do you want to do? Molly asked.

Hopefully, eat—if we can get a waitress. I flagged down a waitress.

Claire laughed.

What are you having?

You choose for me. She smiled at me, and my heart melted.

We'll have catfish curry and spring rolls.

I've never had catfish curry.

You'll love it.

We'll also have iced Thai coffee, Claire said.

I've never had that.

Are you graduating this spring? Molly persisted.

I hope to, I said. My uncle is getting tired of funding me.

What kind of work are you looking for?

I don't know. I haven't settled on any one thing yet.

Have you been to any interviews?

None besides this one, I told her.

I'm sorry. I don't mean to pry.

Well, if you study English, Regina said, picking up the thread of the conversation, you have two choices: teaching or law.

He could also do business, Claire chimed in. There are a lot of English majors, I've noticed, who get their MBAs and go into business.

My fiancé, for instance, Marisa said. He's going to Harvard with me in the fall. He just finished his thesis on Trollope. Have you ever read Trollope, Gideon?

I haven't. His books are too long.

I feel big books are such a commitment.

Exactly, I said.

THE CATFISH CURRY was served along with the iced coffee. I took a sip of coffee from the straw. Claire said, Here—let's switch. You drink from mine. I'll drink from yours. We switched, and then Claire informed me that Marisa was getting married just after graduation.

I'm one of the bridesmaids, she said. You can be my date. It's a black-tie affair, so you'll need a tux. Do you have one? It's going to be wonderful—two hundred and fifty guests and the Sapphires are playing the wedding. Have you heard of them?

Are they a band or a bunch of singing jewelers?

She laughed.

The Sapphires, Marisa said. They're a terrific thirty-piece band from Memphis. We're really lucky to get them. The wedding is downtown at the Ritz. I had wanted to get married in Columbia, but with all the kidnappings, we didn't want to take any risks.

Her bridal shower is next month at the Four Seasons.

Are you nervous? I asked.

About what? The Four Seasons?

No, about the Four Sapphires.

There's no need for nerves if you're marrying the right person, Claire said, intuiting my question.

But how do you know if someone's right for you? I asked.

Molly smiled and looked over at Regina, and together they both looked at me as if I were a fool for doubting the possibility of finding a suitable mate.

Everyone knows that Marisa and Jeremy are right for each other. Wait until you see them together.

Which reminds me, Marisa said, looking at her watch, I've got to go meet Jeremy right now at the Commons. He's taking me to a show.

I have to go too, Regina said. She nudged Molly. Are you coming?

I have a calc exam, Molly said. She apologized: Sorry, I think they're telling me I must go.

They left a substantial tip on the table, and all three smiled in unison: first to me, then, approvingly, to Claire.

It was a pleasure, Regina said. I'm sure we'll be seeing more of you. She extended her hand. I held it from the tips of her fingers as if it belonged to the queen. She held onto my hand a bit longer and gave it a tight squeeze, and then on a whim, I gallantly bowed my head and gave her hand a tender kiss. Remarkably, she blushed. Molly and Marisa said farewell from afar by waving their hands at me, and then clicking their heels, they turned and departed.

We were suddenly left alone amidst empty glasses, plates, and soiled napkins.

How's your catfish?

I'm loving it, Claire said. The curry's a little powerful. It clears the sinuses, don't you think?

I agree, I said.

The coffee is not as good here as it is at Siam. There the coffee-to-cream ratio is more precise.

I agreed again, though I'd never had iced coffee at the Siam. I took a sip and smiled. I think your friends hated me.

No they didn't.

Don't get me wrong: your friends are lovely. But the conversation was awful.

They liked you.

They vetted me. As to liking, I'm not convinced.

It's natural they should "vet" you. They're my best friends. They have to look out for me.

I'm still not convinced.

Oh, you'll see. They're really quite wonderful girls, my best friends. I wouldn't change them for anything in the world.

AND THAT ABOUT DOES the dialogue part. Now for the sex part.

AFTER DINNER WE WENT back to her apartment, which she was sharing with two roommates. Dick and Tom were graduate students: one was a philosophy student (disheveled), and one was a chemist (neat). We sat on her couch together, holding hands, watching Dan Rather intone the news. Dick was eating beans (the eternal food of graduate students), and Tom was carefully sipping tea, half watching Dan Rather, half reading a chemistry book. When I asked him how he could watch TV and study chemistry at the same time, he told me with some pride: I'm inherently a multitasker.

He is, Dick confirmed. Some people are bipolar. Tom is bi-hemispheric. He can work two separate parts of his brain at the same time.

Sounds like a time-saving device. You should patent it.

Oh, it is. I'm highly productive.

It seemed odd to me that both Dick and Tom should be so blasé about having Claire in their company, but that's the thing I soon discovered about Claire: she had a knack for disarming people and putting them at ease.

After a moment we went to her room for privacy. She just squeezed my hand and matter-of-factly said, Come on—see my room.

Neither Tom nor Dick batted an eye.

SHE SHUT THE BEDROOM DOOR behind her. We ripped our clothes off as fast as we could and merged our two nakednesses together. I felt like a camel visiting water after a long drought. She was so very lovely and aggressive. I worked silently, the bed banged beneath us, and she moaned and breathed as if something shocking and revelatory were happening to her, her breathing moving in rhythm with me. She was sexy as hell—I'll give her that—and I came earlier than I should have. But we started right up again, and the second time around I hung in there until she came—the revelation of whatever was happening inside of her suddenly manifest. I wondered what Dick and Tom made of her coming. Who knows, they probably thought nothing of it. They were probably used to it.

AFTERWARD WE LAY THERE in our funk talking. How happy we were naked, our bodies pressed close together! What were my plans, she asked. I told her that I had no real plans, which made her laugh. She loved the novelty of my response. Seriously, she said. And I told her: except for the pursuit of my studies, I was idle—no real plans.

But after you graduate. What do you want to do?

Nothing comes to mind. I haven't really thought about it.

You haven't thought about it? she said.

Well I did think about it for five minutes, and then I got a headache. After that I stopped thinking about it.

Well, unless you're independently wealthy . . .

I'm not.

Then you should give it some thought. You're running out of time. Graduation is near. Don't you want to do something with your life? The sky's the limit.

I suppose I do, I said.

You can be anything you want if you only put your mind to it.

A Marine recruiter once told me the same thing.

Well, how about medicine or law? Do these careers appeal to you?

Not really.

Business?

I suppose.

You'd probably be good at business, she said, looking at me carefully. You've got sangfroid.

Thank you, I said. My parents were reptiles.

Interesting. Mine were socialites.

My condolences.

Seriously, though. What do you want to be?

Myself.

She laughed and said, rather breezily, Don't worry; we can fix that.

What are your plans? I asked.

She placed her hand near my slightly slack erection and stroked my hip. Other than you? For I feel you're becoming one of my plans . . . well, I've got quite a few . . . and thank you for asking. Most guys aren't interested in what a woman's plans are.

You're kidding.

No, it's true!

In this day and age?

I'm not joking. Ask any woman: they'll tell you. Most men don't care what a woman wants to do or even what a woman wants.

I do, I said. Tell me.

Well, I'm majoring in public policy for one. I want to do international work. I want to work in an embassy or something. I'm not sure. But I admire Madeleine Albright immensely. You know, she's a close friend of my grandmother's. And, knowing her, she can only help me in my endeavors. What's more, she's such an inspiration. If it weren't for her, I wouldn't be nearly as motivated as I am. I mean, I owe just that much to Madeleine. Anyway, I was educated at Dalton, and from a very early age, my father provided me with a tutor who'd been educated at Oxford. Her name was Miranda Sommersmith. She taught me French and Italian and art history. When she wasn't tutoring me, she was screwing my dad. I learned this later, of course. But that's a different story. I'm proficient in Russian, Polish, and Lithuanian. I spent my sophomore year of college just outside of St. Petersburg in the dacha of a very famous Russian poet—and I can, as a result, teach you enormous amounts about vodka and Soviet-era poetry. Not all of which is entirely bad. For instance I love the poetry of Mayakovsky. Have you heard of him? He had a tragic love affair that ended in his suicide.

I'll teach you poems. I know many by heart. They just stick in my head like songs.

I can't wait, I said earnestly.

Like this one—it's a fragment that I remember from my Russian poet. It's actually modeled on a stanza from Mayakovsky's "A Cloud in Trousers." It makes a lovely song. What's more, it's dialectical. Here, I'll sing it best I can a cappella:

> My lady in the high tower
> My lady—I call to you from the street—
> Come on down and dance with me and my band
> Or let me through the side gate to share your high
>   tower.

> I can't come down. I can't let you up.
> My bed is a map of tangled sheets.

> But my lady the night is late
> The street is cold

And I—a penitent—honest beyond belief—empty
  pocketed
Can sing of the kingdom far beyond and close
  within
Your girdled gate.

You have a very beautiful voice, I said.

She kissed my clavicle gently.

Besides studying public policy I am also obtaining a minor in Chinese. Have you ever studied it? It is a surprisingly difficult language for me to grasp. I'm naturally gifted at languages, but Chinese is a hard one. I'm third in my class, and I anticipate, if this quarter goes well, especially with my bachelor's paper, to graduate *magna cum laude*, which is a very important credential to get if you're going into embassy work. I'm writing my paper on Tolstoy's theory of history.

I didn't know he had a theory of history, I said.

Well, nobody takes his theory of history seriously—at least not as it's propounded in the final two hundred pages of *War and Peace*. But I think his theory is really quite profound, especially in its focus on the individual. You know, the *principium individuationis*—well, for Tolstoy it was everything.

In a Verdi sort of way, I suppose.

Yes, exactly, she said, laughing. And that's what I'm arguing in my paper. Anyway, this spring, I'm traveling to a monastery in northern France to do human rights work for a Catholic relief agency—and it's not too late for you to join us if you'd like. And then, when I get back from that trip—and after graduating—I have a translating internship that was arranged for me by one of

Ms. Albright's former assistants at the United Nations. Would you like to come to New York this summer? I hope you don't have plans.

I don't. Believe me.

God, I'd love for you to meet my parents.

I'm not much of a socialite.

You'll do fine. You've sangfroid.

When she was done talking, I turned and looked at her face. I saw it in profile. Half in shadow, half cast in light, I couldn't tell whether she was a liar or telling the truth: whether to take her seriously or laugh at the absurdity. Either way, I'd never been with anyone like her.

That would be great, I said.

You can come to France too. I can pay your expenses. I'll have my uncle cover it if necessary.

Whatever. I would love for you to come.

And with that, I did exactly as she commanded.

I SOON DISCOVERED THAT though Claire was enormously intelligent, she nevertheless operated mostly by instinct and intuition. She was suspicious of second impressions, of argument, of reason. (I, on the other hand, operated from a position of stubbornness and reluctance, which was probably no better.) She had standards of taste that she couldn't articulate. She ranked everything she saw. She loved top-ten lists: movies, books, songs, bands, presidents. When she asked me what my top-ten books were, she was appalled when I told her I didn't have any. Do you have a top two? she asked. A top fifty?

What do you want me to say? The Bible and *Hamlet*? The Great Books? Because no, those aren't my favorite two or fifty books.

What are they then?

I've never thought about it that way.

Of course you have.

I haven't, I said, mildly perturbed.

Well, if you were to think about it, which books would you pick? I mean for starters?

I don't know. Books are like people, I said. I like them en masse. I find it hard to pick and choose.

And commit?

What do you mean?

You said you had a hard time committing to long books. Do you also have a hard time committing to people?

Are you asking me to commit?

I may be.

Well, then, I may be willing. But I can't tell you that right now. We have to wait and see.

Wait and see what?

Whether we're right for each other, I suppose.

My opinion, if you don't mind me saying, is that we are right for each other. I've an instinct on you.

And your instincts?

They are almost never wrong. By the way, I also know you have a favorite book. You'll only have to wait and let me prove it!

Good luck, I said. But I don't have favorites.

I do, by the way.

Tell me.

It's a story really, not a book. A short one Tolstoy wrote near the end of his life. I read it twice a year. It grounds me. "Alyosha the Pot" is the story of a hapless peasant boy who gets his nickname because he broke a pot. He falls in love with the merchant's daughter, and when he

seeks to marry her, his father tells him that he will decide when and to whom he will marry. Not long thereafter, the poor hapless boy falls off a roof and dies. It's so
simple and yet filled with such love.

For the merchant's daughter no less. I just hope I don't
fall off the roof when I learn I can't have you.

But you can have me. Just try.

I WAS LEARNING QUICKLY that she trusted her instincts,
and she would grow angry with me because my instincts—my first impressions—often seemed to her to be
lacking in force. If we had a glass of wine, for instance,
we would always discuss it. I would tell her what I had
tasted, and she would tell me what she had tasted—and
I would always revise my opinion of the wine based on
what her palette told me. She thought I lacked confidence, which, to a large extent, I did. Later, after we'd
been dating for several months, she would often grow
furious with me—for I always seemed to be offering
more reasons why we should or shouldn't do something—and she would say: In the amount of time it takes
you to come to a conclusion, we could have already been
out the door doing it.

While we were in bed, after we had made love for the
first time, she told me we would probably be married.
She didn't know how she knew this—only it seemed
clear to her all at once that, together, we would have a
bright future. She'd been with many other guys, she said,
some twice her age, but she'd never had this feeling before. She was alarmingly frank.

What do you think? she asked. How do you like the
word "husband"?

You said you lived with a Russian poet?
Don't be jealous, sweet.
Far from it.
He taught me this, in broken English:

> Stay, O sweet, and do not rise!
> The light that shines comes from thine eyes;
> The day breaks not: it is my heart . . .

So he quoted you poetry, and then you left and broke his heart?

Yes and no. He broke mine first. He used to declaim poetry in the Square of the Musicians. He raged and brooded and laughed through his lines. He was very emotional. He was a sort of performance artist. His name was Rudolph Girst. His parents were revolutionaries, and he inherited their idealism. I liked that about him. He never made a penny for his art, and yet he had dedicated his life to it. He lived on government handouts, and he drove a cab, which was really just his own Peugeot that had hundreds of thousands of miles on it. I fell in love with him after hearing him read in the square. I just happened to be walking through the square, and there he was. He was moved by such passion, and I suppose I wanted him to focus that passion on me, which, of course, he did as soon as he spotted me in the small crowd milling about. He took me back to his dacha, introduced me to all of his artist friends, and that was that. He thought I spoke Russian perfectly. He wanted to come to America with me. I joked and told him he had to first immortalize me in his poetry, which he did. He wrote a whole cycle where I figured simultaneously as muse and the destroyer of inspiration. The poems, if you only knew Russian, are really quite beautiful. Joseph Brodsky called him a huge talent—in the line of Mayakovsky. Rudolph used to declaim poems he wrote of me—of our lovemaking—in the Square of the Musicians. It was very interesting to see me stirring behind the bars of his poetry, like a panther at the zoo. I sat in the square, and yet there I was flashing in the images of his poetry. He was very good at capturing me in the veils of his language.

I don't blame him, I said. If I were a poet, I would write about you too. What happened? How did it end?

He had a problem with alcohol, which, as a rule, I can tolerate to a point. But when he was drinking vodka, he didn't care about me. The same passion he showed in the Square of the Musicians would emerge when he was drunk—the raging, the screaming—only he'd rage and scream at me. He told me that I was ruining his life. He told me that I was making it impossible for him to write poetry, which is crazy because he also told me that I was his muse! He told me I was too American—that I was too interested in money—which, I have to admit, to a certain extent I am. Certainly I'm more interested in money than he was. But I've never been strictly interested in money as money, only as a means to a lifestyle. I like to live comfortably. To have options. When I told him this, he laughed at me. He said, Life is not comfortable for most human beings on earth. Comfort is an illusion perpetrated by American capitalists that drives the rest of the world crazy with longing and envy. He slapped me, saying, This is what life feels like for us. He slapped me again, said: This is how most of us live. Do you like it? He grabbed me by the throat and started choking me. Then he ripped my clothes off—literally ripped them—and then he raped me. When he was through, he zipped his pants and spit at me. There, he said. Welcome to life!

I was gone in the morning, flying back to New York. I never saw him again.

She told me this so matter-of-factly that I was a little taken aback, frightened. Who was I dealing with here? I didn't know what to do or say, and I suddenly felt terrible for her. She went to the bathroom and peed. She came back and, still naked, hugged me. See, I trust you. I've never told anybody that story before. I have an instinct about you. I'm very sure about this.

After that we slept a while or she slept. I looked over at her lying naked next to me in the gray shadows before dawn and was stunned again by her beauty. It made me weak and uncertain. Should I stay or should I go? Should I end it now or follow it through to prove her instincts on me correct? She slept soundly, her face an unruffled mask, her fine black hair pushed away from her forehead, draped behind her on the pillow. She was only inches from my lips, and I wondered how it was possible that this woman whom I'd met only a few hours ago not only claimed me as hers but did so in such a conclusive way that she'd been able to sleep soundly next me as if I'd been, for years, her beloved husband—and not some potentially murderous stranger (which, potentially, I could have been). I reached my hand between her legs, she stirred slightly, and I thought, Now this is mine! With that, I drifted off.

I awoke, suddenly startled. Claire was still asleep. I thought to take a walk and see the sunrise. It was one thing I liked to do, if I could, if I were already awake: watch the sun come up over the lake. I got out of bed, and I was shuffling into my pants when she opened her eyes. Where are you going? I hope this isn't it—a one-night stand.

No, not at all, I whispered. I'm just going for a walk. I'll bring breakfast back in a few hours.

Would you like me to come with you?

No. Get sleep. When you awake, I'll be back and we can take a shower. Then we'll have breakfast.

THE MORNING SUN was beautiful on the lake's horizon. It raised its heavy head—fierce, lionlike. Have you ever stood close to a lion pacing inside its cage? I have, and I was terrified, thinking, What if my bowels should be suddenly ripped open? I have also looked into the mouth of that same lion while it opened and roared, and I felt a primitive fear that made me leap back in terror. I felt that way now, before the rising sun—awed, terrified.

There was a man a stone's throw away from me. He too stood facing the rising sun, stretching, doing his tai chi exercises. I imagined he thought the sun rose because he invited it to do so. I stood with my hands in my pockets wondering what on earth would become of me. I felt loved but aimless. I felt hopeful but despairing. I felt healthy but on the verge of self-destruction. I wanted this moment to last—Claire's and my love—but I wanted it to end. I wanted Claire to trust me, but I was afraid of trust. I wanted to be faithful to her, but I also wanted to destroy this thing, which had come so easily. I hated her Russian poet. I did. But I also understood him—I understood him deep in my heart's core. We were fellow travelers making our marks against the same body and consciousness. I did not understand Claire yet. I was afraid of her and what she meant, but I did not hate her like the poet seemed to hate her. I wanted to dive into cold Lake Michigan and swim to the horizon's edge—swim slowly, cutting the water's surface with my arms as if they were scissors and the lake were a blue silk cloth shimmering in the sun's morning light. I wanted to swim beneath the silk of the water until I disappeared without so much as a trace. And I wanted to tell Claire while doing so that this sense of absence and fullness, which I feel in my heart and I don't know how to account for, is who I most intimately am. I don't know if I am good or bad, monstrous or benign. I also don't want to tell Claire anything of the sort. For it's ridiculous to talk and think in such a way and it's early in the morning and I'm disoriented from lack of sleep.

I was hungry all of a sudden and craved a buttermilk doughnut. I was sexually spent, my dick felt bruised, but I was horny as hell, and right then I had an erection just thinking about Claire and her nakedness and coming in from behind and watching the sun rise off the horizon.

I RETURNED FROM MY WALK and let myself into her apartment. Dick, the philosophy student, was up eating a poached egg over a bowl of granola. He was pimplier than I remembered. He was reading *TV Guide*.

Hello, he said, a bit confused. What are you doing here?

I went to get breakfast, I said, holding up a bag of Dunkin' Donuts. Claire told me to let myself in. This response seemed to irk him, and already I was sorry that Claire was living with two male roommates.

Girls are worse, Claire said when I let myself into her bedroom and got under the sheets with her. I've tried rooming with girls, and either they've had eating disorders, or they've been pathological about men.

I opened the bag of doughnuts, and we began eating them in bed.

I had a roommate, I told her. He was from Puerto Rico. He was so homesick that he used to cry every Friday afternoon for his mother. We shared a bunk. One night he brought a woman home, and I was sleeping in the upper bunk when it started rocking. I woke up confused. There was music from *Star Wars* blaring from the stereo, and when I peaked under to see what was going on, I saw my roommate's back as he drove into her and his girl's eyes wide open, all pupil, like a deer in the headlights, her teeth and fists clenched.

What did you do? She switched position so she was facing me.

What could I do? I said. I just lay there and tried to pretend my roommate wasn't plundering a girl to the military march from *Star Wars*. I imagined instead I was on a ship at sea.

Listening to *Star Wars*?

You're right. It didn't work. I finally just got out bed, put my clothes on, and found a twenty-four-hour diner where I drank weak coffee until morning. When I saw Juan later in the day and joked with him about his escapade, he started crying for his mom. Poor guy, so sentimental.

Claire laughed. I had a roommate. She used to hide cookies everywhere. I would even find them in her shoes. Once I even found them in *my* shoes. But when I confronted her on it, she denied it. I discovered that people who hide cookies hide other things too. They are the worst liars.

I don't hide cookies, I said.

Good. Anyway, she was always telling lies. She told me she came from Venice Beach, which is cool, no doubt. But then I later found out she grew up in a small town outside of Louisville, Kentucky. Which is also cool—if you think about it.

But you don't have to think about Venice Beach.

Even so. I don't know why she would lie about her origins. Anyway, liars—I don't understand them, and that was the problem between her and me. I could never believe anything she told me.

I've told lies too, I said. Nothing serious. But people tell lies. I understand that.

What sort of lies have you told?

I've lied about how and when I lost my virginity.

How did you lose it?

It's nothing.

Please, she said. Do tell.

It's top secret. If I told you I'd have to kill you.

Then please, tell and kill.

No. It's boring. It's part of my mystery.

I'll tell how I lost mine.

I don't know if I'm ready to know.

It really wasn't anything. When I found out my father was sleeping with my tutor, Ms. Sommersmith, I sought revenge. It was stupid. I only punished myself. But I was very reckless. I went into one of those movie theaters and sat next to an old nameless man whose face I could barely make out because it was so dark. That's how I lost it.

Geez.

Anyway, virginity isn't a holy relic. Not worth holding onto. I was glad to get it over with.

So was I.

Tell me how you did it.

In a church.

With a girl?

Yes, of course, a girl! Certainly not a priest!

How old were you?

Not old enough. Neither was she.

Oh, how cute—puppy love.

It was that for sure.

Good for you, she said. I wish I would have started that way. So, any other lies while we're at it?

Nothing serious, I said. My uncle, for instance, asks me time to time if I'm looking for a job. And, to be honest, I haven't yet been to an interview. He's an old guy living out his retirement in Florida with his second wife, and so I usually tell him what he wants to hear. Because sooner or later I will have interviews. I will be looking for a job. It's just that I haven't done that yet.

Well, I've told that type of lie too, Claire said. But that's not the same as lying about something so fundamental as where you came from.

No, I suppose not.

The phone rang. Claire picked up. Hey, Regina! Claire said. Yes, he's right here. Would you like to talk to him? Here, I'll hand him over.

It's Regina, my oldest friend. You met her yesterday at the restaurant. Remember? She wants to say hi to you.

Hi, I said, grabbing the phone.

Hi, she said. I just wanted to see how you guys are doing. You seemed pretty serious last night.

Modestly so, I guess.

Claire's my best friend in all the world. I hope you know that.

So she's said. She's told me a lot about you.

Have you guys slept together?

Yes.

That's nice.

There was a moment of silence.

When can we do that? she asked.

I beg your pardon?

When can we get together? I would like to see you.

I remained silent.

Can you meet me at the Thai restaurant around noon?

Why not?

Thank you, she said. Now, just tell Claire you have plans. She'll understand. She likes to study on Saturdays anyway. Now say to me "Claire's really great" and hand the phone back to her.

Claire's really great, I said. We'll be seeing you. And with that, I handed the phone over to Claire.

He's wonderful, isn't he? Claire said over the phone. We're just getting used to each other. Yes . . . yes . . . OK, bye-bye, darling. Thanks for checking in.

Claire hung up the phone and started kissing me on my neck. That was kind of you to talk to Regina, she said.

It was kind of her to talk to me.

See, she's only looking out for me. We made a pact, when we came here four years ago, to look out for each other. And we've made it, see. We've almost gotten through college together. Without her, I don't know what would have happened to me, but I think I would have broke down like all those other sad cases you hear about.

It's nice to have friends you can count on.

Yes.

Claire positioned herself on top of me, threw her hair back, and started rocking. So what are your plans for today?

No plans, I said. Only you.

Oh, she said. She bent over and kissed me full on the lips. Thank you for saying that, Gideon. But I'm afraid I'm off-limits the rest of the day—unless you come to the library with me. We could take a break from our studies and make love in the stacks. Have you ever done that before?

No. Have you?

Not yet, she said. But we will.

I have to meet somebody for lunch, I said. And then errands. Can we meet again tomorrow?

OK, she said.

With that, our lovemaking became fierce, the bed banging beneath us, and I couldn't believe it, really—that I was with such a lovely woman.

OH YES, I FORGOT to mention. We discussed her top-five doughnuts that morning.

In ascending order, she said: 1.) Bavarian cream, 2.) custard-filled, 3.) whipped cream, 4.) chocolate-filled, 5.) vanilla-filled.

You've got to be kidding, I said. They're all cream-filled doughnuts.

Yep. I love creamy filled doughnuts.

Yep, I said back to her jokingly.

Do you have any favorites? she asked.

I have a feeling this is going to be a trope of our conversations.

I love it, she said. I love comparing favorites. It's a great thing to do. And then, compulsively, she said, I love you. She took a bite of her Bavarian cream and kissed me full on the lips.

OK, I said, wiping the cream from my lips. That doughnut right there is my all-time favorite. I've never had a better doughnut.

See, Gideon, you do have favorites! I only hope I'll become one of them.

I WALKED CLAIRE to the library that morning. It had become overcast and drizzly. A wind from the west, into which we walked, cut right into us. I carried an umbrella down low against the wind, and it nearly snapped on me. That's when I got the idea for Anderson's Windless Umbrella. As we walked into the wind and drizzle, I described it to her. It would be vented around the middle like a parachute with four or five vents, and above the vents would be small nylon flaps to prevent the rain from falling through the vent. Can you picture it? Don't you think it's a wonderful idea? I asked. See, I'm a genius!

It is a good idea actually, she said. Do you know how many umbrellas I throw out during springtime alone?

Actually I've always preferred slickers or just getting drenched like Gene Kelly. Or Pooch.

Pooch? she said.

We had a dog, Pooch, who'd get wet in the rain and stink for a week. She was a longhaired mutt. I spent my first two years of college just like her, getting rained on. Showing up to class drenched to the bone.

And stinky?

Yes.

She grabbed hold of me as we walked. I love your umbrella idea. Seriously. It's a brainstorm.

No, it's a rainstorm.

I'm serious, Gideon. It could be just the thing for you. A start.

It could be, I suppose. But to be honest, it probably won't be. I don't trust big ideas.

But that's just it—it isn't a big idea. It's just the right size.

Well, if it were such a great idea, why hasn't anyone already thought of building a windless umbrella?

Because no one's thought about it until you—just now!

I don't believe it. Umbrellas have been around in one form or another for centuries, and I'm the first to think of it? I don't think so. It's too impractical. I'm sure it wouldn't work.

You never know until you try.

And how am I supposed to try?

You could draft some pictures of your idea and see if you can get it patented.

Too much work, I said. I've got other things.

Like what?

Like just getting through this quarter, graduating.

Do me a favor. Just draw it up. I know people who can help you. My father has connections. He would be able to help you get funding. That's what he does for a living. He takes good ideas and helps nurture them into existence.

Just then our umbrella tore. Jesus! I screamed, for a piece of the umbrella had hit me in the eye.

See, she said, jamming the umbrella in a garbage can that was overflowing with broken umbrellas, you could solve this problem if you put your heart into it.

I couldn't, I said. I'm an English major, not an inventor. I don't have an entrepreneurial bone in my body.

Nonsense. There are plenty of people I could marshal behind you. You could patent it, develop it, and market it. It would be your own company. It's an answer, she said. Oh I'm so happy for you. We were on the steps of the library. You're the kind of person who will succeed despite yourself. You just need some help, that's all.

Let me think about it, I said.

Anderson's Windless Umbrella Company. It's a good start!

We kissed on the steps of the library. Some grad student overburdened with books burst out of the library and almost knocked us down. He turned and scowled as if he'd never seen a couple that was in love before.

I'll think on it, I promised. Honestly, I will.

Make some drawings. That's all I ask. I can run them by my father. But it's absolutely thrilling. With that, she turned and headed into the library, and I turned and headed for home.

THAT'S AS WELL AS I can remember it—dialogue and all. It's 5:00 a.m. Time to knock off for a while. No calls from Claire. I thought she might call . . . my one thought before drifting off. After I had left Claire at the library, the idea of keeping my promise to Regina crept into my head—she of the queenly hand that I had kissed. At first I thought of it as absurd, and I kept heading for home— hup, two three four; hup, two three four—but as way led onto way, and thought led onto thought, and the increasingly affirmative sense that opportunity was something that must be pursued at all costs, especially if it presented itself so innocuously, before I knew it I was retracing my steps—at first with mild hesitation and then, checking my watch and seeing I was almost late, at a trot. I trotted back to that Thai restaurant. Sure, there were twinges of guilt, but they were easily rationalized away. We've only been together less than twenty-four hours, Claire and I. Surely she doesn't possess me yet. This was followed by a deeper twinge of guilt. This is ostensibly her best friend, and they had promised never to betray each other, and now here I was on the cusp of forcing that betrayal, and, look, here it was even worse since it was a three-way betrayal. What about Claire's instincts that we were to be married? What if, on a lark, she were correct? Wouldn't this dalliance, this abdication of fidelity forever undermine our union, but then of course, I would think how absurd it was to worry about such things. We live but once (I was running now), not twice, and before I knew it I was in the restaurant with Claire's best friend, Regina. (Heck, I almost forgot her name but luckily upon seeing her it came to me in an instant.) She wore jackboots, had butch hair, and sported a sleeveless T-shirt with army surplus cargo pants. We barely said a word, and without eating a thing (come on, let's get out of here, she said, panting in my ear) she grabbed my hand, and we were out the door and headed to her place, which was in this loft space on Sixty-Third Street that she shared with two mutts and a half-dozen or so black-and-white kittens, and who knows, maybe a roommate or two who chose her pad to flop down in.

What I remember of that simple afternoon tryst is this: Regina was a painter.

She painted huge canvasses of empty rooms filled with the most beautiful light imaginable. It was a light at the end of the tunnel kind of light. A light that you see when you die and go to heaven kind of light. Ask her what she painted, and she'd tell you, I paint light. But when you saw one of her pictures it was clear she was attempting nothing short of depicting some sort of celestial bliss. The beauty of the light in her pictures was so urgent and raw, it produced a lump in my throat.

Well, are you going to bore me to tears and admire my art?

What did you have in mind?

I want you to fuck me silly. I want you to fuck me until my eyeballs roll around in my head. I want you to fuck me until a beam of light comes shooting out my mouth. Do you think you can do that for me?

I can try.

Now get over here, Gideon. Turn me on, and let me show you the light.

She was fat, with a big round ass. Tattoos of names and numbers—algebra, calculus, a shibboleth of numeric data that added up to some algorithm with runic import—proliferated in inky darkness across the canvas of her body. She wore a ring on her pinky toe, which, at one point, I found myself sucking. She had a ring in her nose as well, which I tugged. I watched her shake and giggle, and it made me giggle, and it was by giggling and jiggling that we passed the rest of the afternoon in the light of those glorious paintings, and when we were done and I began to drift off post-coitus, something happened that

I didn't expect: she kicked me—literally kicked me out of bed, her heels driving into my thighs, bruising them, and before I had a chance to react she kicked me again with full force and heels against my lower spine. I thought I heard a cracking sound, a shifting of spinal alignment, and I felt a tremendous pain—so much so that I turned around and before I knew what I was doing I clouted her not once but twice straight to the face with a right and then a right again.

There was blood gushing out of her nose, and a tooth gashed the skin on my knuckle. With that, I gathered my stuff, and without saying good-bye, started for the door. I heard her shout after me you asshole or something of the sort, to which I rebutted, You almost broke my god-damned back! To which she shouted, You think you can escape me? I turned and told her I thought I could.

Well, you can't, she screamed loudly enough so that her voice could be felt in the temples of my skull.

When I got back to my apartment I applied Mercuro-chrome with the little glass-knobbed applicator to my knuckles to keep them from getting infected from her saliva (I irrationally thought she might have rabies), and sometime the next day I ran into Claire again, and she asked how I had hurt my hand, and I told her, caught off-guard, I don't remember. I don't know if she put two and two together when she saw Regina, but the whole in-cident was never mentioned again even though Regina never did anything to hide the welt on her face where I had hit her.

On bad weather days I still feel the hurt in my lower back. I don't know what Regina told Claire—though I imagine she told her the worst, and if she did it's to

Claire's credit, I suppose, that she never brought the issue up or held it against me. She probably should have, and in retrospect I'm sad for Claire that she didn't.

Ever since that day, Regina hated me. She was a malevolent force, a dark cloud—a stygian black hole of night—that always threatened to bring discord and ruin to whatever occasion might bring the three of us together. Our eye contact always suggested exactly what she had predicted: I couldn't escape her. She knew more than anyone else exactly who I was and what dark things I was capable of, and in that way, she proved prescient.

Unbelievably to me, Regina's paintings never found a legitimating outlet. She exhibited in neither gallery nor museum, nor did she ever appear to find a sponsor for her work. I hadn't seen the likes of her paintings, which were absolutely glorious, until, some time later, Claire and I were at the Tate in London where we saw the late works of Turner. It was only then that I realized that Regina was a kindred spirit of Turner's.

IT WAS ON THOUGHTS of this betrayal to Claire that I finally fell asleep. I woke several times from bad dreams, alarmed, disoriented. A faint smell of sulfur was in the air, and I couldn't decide whether it was coming from outside, from the apartment below, or from Satan. Did he suddenly appear in the corner of the room to smile on my progress? Who knows? I grew up in a mostly Catholic neighborhood, and unlike many of my Catholic brethren, I never could believe in Satan. In fact, I despised hearing weekly renditions of hell in our priest's sermons. He was quite obsessed with the place. You don't want to go there, he would tell us. Trust me.

It was worse at funerals where we fervently prayed that the soul of the departed went northward to heaven, not south to Dixie and the fiery lakes of hell. We lived in a cash-strapped parish, so whenever the priest wasn't holding forth on the temptations of Satan, he pulled out and polished his favorite sermon: It is easier for a camel to get through the eye of the needle than a rich man to get through the gates of heaven. Give what you can to the parish and be spared the fate of the rich man—who, presumably, ended up in the fiery lakes of hell. For three years, I was an altar boy, what we in the trade called a bell ringer, and if we failed to jingle our bells at the moment of the transubstantiation, then Father Henley would gaze at us with a sort of perturbed disdain that gave me some idea of what Satan might look like, should he indeed exist.

I loved Satan as he was pictured in the *Children's Illustrated Bible* circa 1973. He seemed like a Marvel Comics superhero—monstrous and fiery red with two shocking horns poking out of his head. In a famous picture of that same Bible, the devil as superhero stood on a cliff with Jesus, who was depicted, by contrast, as a sort of pale bureaucrat—bearded and in flowing robes. Satan was tempting Jesus to jump off the cliff to prove that angels would rescue him. But Jesus declined, even as angels were descending to his aid. He wouldn't back down. We as children were asked to take sides with Jesus, but it was impossible. Satan was just too cool with superhero muscles and his pointed horns. I dare you to jump. I dare you to will your innermost desire. I dare you to let your desire be consummated. Forget about the consequences. Please let it be consummated.

I lost my virginity at the church I went to, Saint Joseph the Worker. I was an altar boy, and she was a choir girl. Her name was Deanna Mills. For a while in my nascent adolescence I worshipped at her altar. She was lovely, slender and tender (as I imagine Joan of Arc might have been), and we were both curious about the strange physical mysteries the other harbored. We had kissed several times leading up to the event, and I, courageously, had felt her up. That's when we knew. It was before the six-thirty mass one February morning. We both had arrived early with nothing to do, the priest was still sleeping or saying his matins or eating Cheerios or doing whatever else priests do in the early morning hours. In any event, he hadn't arrived yet in the chapel. We, on the other hand, both arrived on our bikes, our hands raw with cold from the metal handlebars, our mutual gowns flowing behind us—as if we were those angels descending to Jesus's aid in that picture from my old *Children's Illustrated Bible*. I had a key to the church, which I had borrowed for just this purpose. We let ourselves in, locking the heavy door behind us. I unlocked another door to a small chapel that wouldn't be used for Sunday mass. She boldly suggested that we do it on the altar near the sacristy. I was superstitious about getting too close to the sacristy, but when she said, Why not? I capitulated. I was always capitulating, I now realize. We tentatively stepped out of our gowns and the pedestrian clothes we wore underneath. Though she didn't need one, she wore a bra. She took it off, for she didn't want me messing with it. She told me with pride that she had started menstruating six months earlier. I nodded solemnly, as the occasion demanded. It was a brief, strange, holy encounter. She laughed through clenched teeth, as did I. We bumped the sacristy, the doors popped open, and some of the holy chalices tumbled out, to my horror. When we were finished, I carefully replaced the chalices back in the sacristy. I said a Hail Mary for good measure and crossed myself. She rang the transubstantiation bells to mark the occasion.

Thank god that's over, she said with a maturity that was beyond her years. I agreed wholeheartedly. Then we laughed as if we had both sloughed off the oppressive weight of a lifelong virginity.

THE MORNING AFTER Claire's ultimatum and my subsequent sleepless night filled with these rambling thoughts and scattered nonsensical mental images, I showered and I walked over to Valois, a "see your food" steam-tray cafeteria. Everything looked good and I was feeling hungry, so I ordered enough food for six people. I had three eggs sunnyside up, sausage patties, a round of Canadian bacon, grits, pancakes, and French toast. I was hungry. I ordered a half pint of milk, a glass of apple juice, and a cup of coffee. The coconut cream pie was tempting, so I ordered that as well. I carried the tray of food to an open table, and the kitchen staff carried my beverage tray. I sat there alone at my table, hunched over my food. I buttered my toast, salted my eggs, poured syrup on my French toast and pancakes and began eating. I was hungry and exhausted. A pretty woman asked if she could share my table. By all means, I said. Sit. She looked at both trays and wondered aloud if there was someone else coming to join me. No, they're both mine, but please—go ahead, sit down. She had a hard-boiled egg and a piece of toast.

She was drinking a cup of tea. My eyes were red-rimmed and sandpapery. My furnace was empty and in need of fuel. I was depressed and in search of happiness. We went back and forth with the social pleasantries. Where are you from? What do you do for a living? I was too hungry to talk much. I mostly listened, and what do you know—she started talking about leaving Hyde Park. She was going to New York where she'd just landed a job at a Madison Avenue advertising agency. She was leaving tomorrow. She had been in Hyde Park for only three years. It's a wonderful town, she mentioned, but it's no place to get stuck. It was a stepping stone, didn't I agree? Of course I agreed. How could I say no? It was a university community after all. Yes, yes, I said. I continued to eat. New York City was the place to go and be somebody. A sadness was gnawing away at me. Gluttony would be my cure. When I was done eating, I wiped my soiled fingers on a napkin. I dipped the end of the napkin into a glass of water and washed the sticky stuff that had gotten smeared on the corner of my mouth. I thanked the lady for her company and wished her luck. Bon voyage, I said, reaching out to shake her hand, and then, politely, I belched.

When I got home I called Claire and told her it was over. I was a pig, a beast. I wasn't worth wasting her precious time on. She had ambition, determination, goals. I had none of these things. Go to New York for god's sake and leave me alone. I hope you make it to your destination. I hope you one day end up being Madam Secretary of State. I shall have the television on as you get appointed, and I will cheer your fortune. I know you will move on and one day none of this will even be remembered. But remember this: I did love you. I loved you for your lists, for your ambition for being everything that I am not. Now let me live and rot in peace. I want nothing at all to do with any of it!

There was silence on the other end. It was the silence before a bomb went off. I don't know what had come over me, but I was sick of it all: the lists, the need to do, to be. I just wanted to be left alone. There was a sob. Did I hear a little sob? Maybe it sounded like a sob, although she wasn't altogether the sobbing type. But there was distinctly a throat clearing, and then she said, Thank you, Gideon.

Thank you for what?

Thanks for finally being honest with me. With that, she hung up, and I said into the space in front of me, So long.

After I hung up the phone with Claire, I took a long, satisfying, indolent shit. I had nothing else to do all day except get the mail. So there I sat, on the pot, taking a long dump. I sat there long enough to read half a novel. I wiped, flushed the toilet, went downstairs to check the mail, and, like clockwork, there it was—another check from my uncle with a note that read, quite simply, as follows:

> Gideon,
> To tide you over some until I get the plan.
> Love always,
> Unc.

My father was fond of telling me that I didn't have what it takes to get by in this world. Who knows? Perhaps he's right. You'll never amount to anything, he would say in disappointment. I was his third son, and as far back as I can remember, he thought I was a failure. He blamed it on my mother. You've inherited her genes, he liked to tell me, and then he would add, without humor, You certainly haven't inherited any of mine.

However, if it's any consolation—and I'm sure it was to my father—my two brothers went into the family business, and they have been very successful. I followed the second son by six years. There was a ten-year difference between the oldest and me. Because I was so much younger than they, we never really hit it off as brothers. I was treated, from the first, as a second-class citizen. The fact that my mother was the only one in the house who had any hope for me didn't help matters. It was a household run by men, and her views were definitely subordinate to my father's and my brothers' views.

I was never very active as a child. I'd lay around all day not doing much of anything, and it used to drive my father furious. Why don't you go out and play. Surely you must have some friends to play with.

Fact is, I had very few friends growing up. I wish, retrospectively, that I had had more. But I didn't. Actually, part of the problem was asthma, so I never liked to go outside and play. Another problem was there just weren't many kids in my neighborhood. The friends I chose tended to be sedentary like me. Unfortunately I was so sedentary that finding other sedentary friends was rather a bit of a challenge. Now that I look back, letting memory do the sorting, I see that most of my childhood friends barely made an impression on me one way or the other. I recall that after a certain point I just gave up on birthday parties (both going to and asking for them). Birthday parties forced me to play with a mix of kids whom I invariably didn't like. I felt trapped in crowds, misunderstood. I didn't fit in. On the other hand, I didn't care to fit in. I was a nervous, self-conscious boy. I was gangly, uncoordinated. I laughed at inappropriate times and openly cried when moved by evidence of strong emotion in others. Great human endeavor, for instance, tended to make me cry. I could watch a sprinter on the track team, and there I'd be at the finish line moved to tears by the emotion of such great human effort. Other kids didn't like me or understand me, or they thought I was a bit off. OK. That was just fine as far as I was concerned. But when my mother, who, like me, was also awkward in social situations, asked me to do my best and get along with others, I would say, Why? It was a rather insolent thing to say, but I didn't see the point back then, even as a kid, of killing myself trying to fit in.

What's the point? I would ask my mom, who, despite her pretenses to the contrary, felt similarly. She, like me, had very few friends.

Oh there is a point to fitting in. Believe me, Gideon. You will win more friends.

I don't want more friends.

You must want more friends. Everybody wants more friends.

I don't, I said defiantly. And I don't think you do either, or else you would have more. It was a cruel thing to say to my mom, but I couldn't help myself. She stood there stunned, not knowing what to do or say. After a moment, she resorted to bewildered pity. Oh, poor boy, she said, patting my head.

A COUPLE OF CHILDHOOD FRIENDS did make an impression. Hal Berkowitz was a great pal. Unfortunately he was prone to abusing cats and other living creatures. I was friends with him for four years—between the ages of ten and fourteen. I should have taken his abuse of animals for a bad omen and avoided him, but I didn't. Looking back, I don't see why I was so attracted to him. We had nothing in common. He was a violent, modestly insane dolt. What's more, I happened to like animals and felt devastated every time he decided to torture one of his cats. He'd swing them around his head like a lasso and let them fly off into the yard squealing. Once he accidentally let one fly off into a brick wall, and when the cat didn't move (was he paralyzed? dead?), Hal took his big black boot and squashed him just like that underfoot. It was horrible. I was horrified. Hal, however, didn't think much about it. He merely scraped the animal up and threw him in the garbage. So much for nine lives, he said.

I never could guess what he told his parents when they asked him where the cat was. Nevertheless, I kept hanging out with him. I found him extremely beguiling. He had courage of a sort that attracted and repelled me at the same time. When he wasn't flinging cats, he was actually a pretty nice guy. We usually talked girls. Our tastes in them diverged considerably. He was an ass man and preferred blondes. I, on the other hand, hadn't yet formulated an opinion on what I liked. Besides girls, we also shared an interest in the Steve Miller Band. We loved his sound, and his lyrics spoke to us where we lived—I really like your peaches, want to shake your tree. It was a music that was surreal, low-key, and cool all at once. We'd play Steve Miller tapes and hang out in Hal's garage where his father had a device for making shotgun shells. We spent hours handmaking 12-gauge shotgun shells. There we would work with highly dangerous explosives, absorbed in our task, talking about things that adolescent boys invariably talk about when they don't realize they are even talking. We'd insert the primer into the base of the shell, add gunpowder, then tamp down the wad and fill it to the top with 6-shot. We'd put the shell into the device, which was like a lemon juicer, and we'd pull down on the handle. Presto—just like that—we'd have a shotgun shell. We'd make piles of them, store them in old Remington boxes, and his dad would go off and shoot them when he had a chance at the local gun club.

His father worked the day shift at a factory that made fire extinguishers, and his mom worked the night shift at the same factory. We never saw much of either of them, and when I did see one or the other of them, I was always startled by their age: they seemed as old as grandparents. One episode I'll never forget. Hal had been complaining of a toothache for weeks, and nothing had been done about it. One afternoon I was at his house, and I was surprised to see his dad home. It was one of the few occasions I ever saw Hal's old man. Daddy, I want to go to the dentist. My tooth hurts.

Which one? Show me.

This, he said, pointing with his finger.

Go get me a piece of string.

No, Hal said. I want the dentist to do it.

Get me a string. We're not going to the dentist.

When Hal refused to get a string, his father disappeared and returned a moment later with some kite string, the end looped off in a slipknot. Come here, his father said.

Hal refused.

Get over here.

Hal looked over at me, then at his dad. I want the dentist to do it.

Forget it, his father said. A dentist is out of the question. With alarming speed and force, he snatched Hal, got him in a headlock, and proceeded to strangle Hal until he turned blue. He pinned Hal's head to his knee and forced his jaw open by driving his thumb and forefinger into Hal's jaw muscle. He slipped the string over the tooth, muttered, We're not going to a dentist's over this, then yanked the string with tremendous ferocity. The tooth flew across the room. Hal started screaming. There was blood all over the place. I felt as invisible as a ghost all of a sudden, and, like a ghost, I got up quietly from where I sat in astonishment and slipped out of their house, undetected. I remember saying to myself on the way home, So much for nine lives.

IT'S BECAUSE OF HAL that I have a tattoo on my forearm. He had read a book on how to self-tattoo, and we tattooed each other with ink drawn from blue and red BIC ink cartridges that we pulled from the clear plastic tubes of the pens. I attempted to make a sketch of an eagle gripping a branch with its powerful claws, but the illustration was poorly executed by Hal, and the tattoo turned out to look like a big inky lump on my forearm. It's disgusting, and I hate to look at it even now, but Hal and I were caught up in the moment. He was also the guy who tempted me to do drugs. We'd sit in the rafters of his garage on a piece of plywood. Spread out before us would be a large Turkish hookah and other implements of smoking paraphernalia that he'd obtained at a head shop. He'd pack the bowl full of marijuana that he had obtained from a Baggie in his mother's top dresser drawer. He'd light up and encourage me to smoke, but I always declined, which was just fine with him. He thought peer pressure was generally a real drag. I got high, nevertheless, on the secondhand smoke. We'd sit around in his funky little attic in the garage telling stupid jokes and laughing like idiots while the Steve Miller band played on his portable tape recorder: I'm a joker. I'm a toker. I'm a midnight smoker. Retrospectively, I can say this: it was fun hanging out with Hal. Eventually he'd pull out a stack of his father's yellowing *Playboys*. It was the first time I had seen pictures of naked ladies, and, believe me, it was more potent than any drug. Hal was the guy who misinformed me (I believed him at the time) that the large-breasted women of *Playboy* all eventually killed their husbands by suffocating them with their breasts. He called them Black Widows, and he argued that it would be the ideal way to go. If only to have them in bed once . . . I'd sacrifice my life for that! I supposed at the time that I would have too.

Hal almost sacrificed his life for a lot less. It was during the last spring of our friendship when, inexplicably, he attempted to commit suicide by taking a bunch of heart pills. I didn't know what heart pills were at the time, though I imagined they were red and heart-shaped— like those Brach's red-hot candies that my uncle had purchased for me on the day of my First Communion when we saw all the tourist sites.

When I heard the news of Hal's attempted suicide and his hospitalization (his mother had called my mother to explain what happened), I hopped on my bike and pedaled in the roadside gravel nearly ten miles to Sisters of Mercy where he had a room in the psychiatric ward. When I entered the room, I was shocked that he was all alone, no visitors. There weren't any flowers, get-well cards, balloons, or other items of cheer and sympathy. I sat on the chair across from him, and we started telling stupid jokes back and forth. He said that, though it looked like suicide, he was really just experimenting with drugs. He told me how his stomach had been pumped and how his dad had lost it when he came and saw what state his son was in. He started screaming at Hal—berating him for doing such a stupid thing. It was so bad, the nurses tried to calm him, but when his father wouldn't be calmed down, they kicked him out, and he'd subsequently been banned from the hospital, which is why Hal had no visitors—because when his dad had been banned from the hospital, his mother had been banned by his dad. It's an evil cycle, Hal said placidly. Hold one side down, and all sides are held down in turn.

I had smuggled a tape recorder into his room, and I put a Steve Miller tape on low volume. I want to fly like an eagle till I'm free, fly like an eagle, let my spirit carry me. I asked what it was like when he was dying, and he told me that it made him feel free. You know, how when you go down a sledding hill and you feel a rush?

Yeah.

Well, something like that. Time keeps on slipping, slipping, slipping into the future. Like you're going down the sled. First you feel the rush, then everything slows down, and then for a while you don't know what's happening because you forget that part, and then after that, a white light. When I opened my eyes, I was in the hospital with an oxygen mask on my face and a tube in my throat, and I didn't know what was going on.

Did you feel like you were being suffocated—like with the Black Widows?

Yes, it was very similar to what a Black Widow would do to you.

By the way, I said, trying to cheer him up, I think I saw a Black Widow yesterday.

Where?

I saw her at the 7–Eleven. She was wearing this mink, so it was hard to tell what her breasts looked like. But one thing is for sure—she was naked beneath the mink.

Cool, he shouted, nearly out of his mind.

Yeah. She was sexy.

I don't believe it.

I didn't either. But there I was in the 7–Eleven, and in she walks off the street wearing this mink.

How did you know she was a Black Widow?

There was something about her, I said. I mean, the mink and no clothes underneath. Who else could it have been?

Did you go up to her and say anything? I mean, you could have seen her breasts.

No.

You fool, Anderson, he said, sitting up in bed. Then, echoing my father, he shook his head with disappointment. You know, your problem, Anderson, is you don't have what it takes. You need courage. Hell, I would have gone up to her and asked her to marry me. What would I have to lose? She might have gone to bed with me.

She might have, I said.

But, look, courage is what got me here. Which 7–Eleven was it?

The one down the street.

And did she have a nice ass?

Yeah, it was nice.

While we sat there talking, the phone never rang once, nor were there any other visitors. At the end of the afternoon, I got up to go.

Well, I said, I should be going.

Thanks, Anderson, Hal said. Thanks for visiting. I appreciate it.

No problem.

Well, if you want to forget you know me after this incident, I wouldn't blame you.

What are you talking about?

I wouldn't blame you if you stopped seeing me. You probably think I'm crazy.

I don't, I said.

But if you did, I wouldn't blame you. I would never blame you.

Don't worry. We're pals.

All right, but remember, if that should change, no hard feelings.

There was an uncomfortable silence, and then he said, Bye.

Bye, Hal, I said.

Bye, Anderson.

We shook hands, and then I stepped outside the hospital. It was dark and raining. Against my better judgment, I rode my bike all the way home, sloshing through the roadside gravel and splashed by cars.

I lost track of Hal after eighth grade. He was right: I just naturally wanted to stop hanging out with him, and I couldn't explain why that was. Incidentally, I also lost an interest in the Steve Miller Band, though when I occasionally hear one of his songs on the radio, it invariably puts me in mind of all those lost hours Hal and I spent in his garage making so many shotgun shells and theorizing on the lifestyles of Black Widows. To this day, I don't know what's become of Hal, but I wouldn't be surprised if he was: a.) dead; b.) in jail for being a serial killer; c.) homeless and wandering the streets in a drug-addled haze; or d.) superintendent of the local school system.

I HAD ANOTHER FRIEND, Vance Ignaffio, who was a tuba player in the band. His father was in the apparel business, and apparently he had mob connections. I was rather awed by this fact. Since Vance never made a big deal about the mob connections, I assumed it was true. Other signs conspired to corroborate my belief that Vance's family was mob-affiliated. For one, Vance was obsessed with the music of Frank Sinatra. For two, Vance was often driven to school in a long Lincoln Continental with tinted windshields. For three, as nearly as I could tell, Vance never told a lie.

Vance was a portly, misshapen boy with large dark

rings around his eyes. He breathed out his mouth and seemed always to be struggling for breath (like me, with my asthma). Nevertheless, he managed to have girls all over the place. I think he was popular with the girls because he exuded something I and countless others have never been able to obtain: effortless self-confidence. He was like a duck—things rolled off his back. He didn't give the slightest damn about anyone's opinion. He was fat, but who gives a fuck? He was ugly, but he wasn't bothered by it. He was stupid—so what? He could care less. Later, when he was universally reviled for a horrible thing he'd done, he wasn't bothered by it. He was amazingly unflappable. He chalked it up to other people's ignorance. They hate me because they don't have the guts to be like me. Such statements coming from him were common, and they invariably made me laugh. He was the funniest guy I ever met, and I think it was his self-confidence, more than anything, that I found so unsettlingly funny. He nicknamed me Laugh Track. His blandest assertion—it's cold out there, Anderson, why don't you wear a hat!—seemed hilarious to me, and I would snort uncontrollably with a combination of laughter and I don't know what. I've never met a person since who could make me laugh like he could.

Of all his sundry girlfriends (and I asked him to loan me a few, but he never did) he was most obsessed with a rather unattractive girl who was preternaturally shy. She recoiled at the slightest eye contact. She was a shrinking violet if there ever was one. She was docile and seldom said a word. Vance was always ordering her about, and she was always following his orders. It was a weird dynamic they had established and a sorry sight to watch, but I laughed at the whole thing because Vance had a way with orders that were funny, and it was funny watching her capitulate in her terrified way. I never suspected how deep his connection to her was until crude photographs he'd snapped were passed around the school cafeteria for all to see. Under the gleam of a florescent bulb in a windowless cinder-block practice room, he had compelled her to pose nude in all sorts of graphic positions with all sorts of phallic things inserted into her orifices. He then snapped Polaroids of her—fifty-two to be exact, a deck of cards. They were terrifying, humiliating pictures made more terrifying by the crudeness of the photography. She was gritting her teeth in every shot as if she were being bludgeoned by the camera. Her eyes were red as if she'd been crying. A rash formed around her neck and cheeks. I remember when I saw them, I was so appalled that I immediately wanted to forget them. But the images of her remain vividly impressed upon my memory to this day. When the school authorities caught up with Vance, I think they wanted to publicly hang him. Instead, he was suspended for two weeks. Had he been anyone else (other than a mobster's son), he probably would have been kicked out and banned forever from school premises, but I'm sure his dad or some other henchman made an offer the principal could not refuse.

When Vance returned after his suspension, public opinion had caught up with him. Had he been a leper in Calcutta, he couldn't have been more shunned. (The shy girl was also shunned.) Even I was embarrassed to be seen near Vance, lest others think I was in on his prank. So, like everyone else, I shunned him too. It was not long after the picture incident when I repeated my experience at the church with another choir girl, Maria Juarez. Maria and I were alone together cleaning up the main chapel after the twelve o'clock mass. Our job was to clean the chalices, wash out the little bottles of wine and water, polish the communion plates and chalices, and generally clean up by putting choir books and missalettes in their proper places. While we were cleaning up, Maria asked me if I had anything to confess. I didn't know what she was talking about, but I secretly sensed that she was referring to my escapade with Deanna. It hadn't occurred to me that Deanna would talk about what had happened between us. I certainly wasn't inclined to share the details of the event, but if Deanna had talked and spilled the beans to Maria, then maybe—if I judge the tone of Maria's question correctly—she was not only referencing common knowledge between us but, with the slightly curious lilt to her question, wondering if she'd suddenly met a guy brave enough to go on a similarly brazen adventure with her. Nevertheless, I wasn't ready to admit anything, so I told her: I have nothing at all to confess.

Oh yeah? Maria said, smiling at me, carefully polishing the chalice. She had pretty white gloves on her hands so as not to leave any fingerprints. That's not what I've heard.

What did you hear? I asked, suddenly flustered and possibly curious as well.

I heard that you and Deanna did it.

Who told you?

Well, if you're not talking—and I presume you're not, otherwise you would have something to confess—that only leaves one other witness.

Deanna? Did Deanna tell you?

With that, she set the chalice down and walked over to me and placed those pretty, white-gloved hands of hers on my chest. She lifted up her pretty lips, and I stared into her eyes as if I were standing on the edge of a cliff. Go ahead, the devil himself seemed to plead: Jump. And so, with nothing else to do, I jumped off the cliff and into the puddle of her eyes.

Come, Maria said. Let's not do it here. Certainly there must be somewhere more private.

I don't know any place more private than this.

Yes, but what if the priest should walk in? We need something more secluded.

OK. Where?

How about over there? She pointed with her gloved hand. How about the confessional? Let's try it in there. Don't you think that would be fun?

I do.

The confessional was cramped for the two of us, but so are most clandestine places one finds to perform this business.

She asked me to confess.

I have nothing to confess.

Oh please, Gideon. Everyone has something to confess. If you confess it to me not only do I promise not to tell anyone, but I promise to forgive you if it's forgiveness you're asking for.

I don't know what to say.

Please try something.

I don't have anything to say.

OK, let me show you how. Unlike Deanna, I'm not a virgin. This is not my first time. The first time I did it was when I was twelve years old.

I see.

So what do you have to say?

Only this: can we stop with the questions? I'm not the confessing type.

Oh sure you are, Gideon. You just haven't learned how to unburden yourself. But one day you will. I promise you. I can tell just by looking into your eyes. I can read what's written on your soul.

What does it say?

It says you are lazy. It says you like me. You like me very much.

With that, she lifted her shirt—there was her nut-brown skin, pretty against the white cloth of the vestment—and she smothered me with tender affection.

AFTER THAT NOTABLE ESCAPADE, I remember wanting to tell Vance—to confess—all about how I had gotten lucky at church not once but twice. But such was not to be. Our days of confessing our stories to each other were over. A few awful pictures and peer pressure had gotten between us.

Occasionally I'd see him in the school hallway, walking alone. It was terrible what he'd done. I'd look at him for signs that he was cracking under the pressure of being a social pariah, but he was so damned confident and unflappable that it was water off his back. Occasionally he would yell over to me when we passed in the hallway. I'm sure my behavior—ignoring him—made him sick. The shy girl—cornered and seemingly without options—stuck with him. The school authorities didn't allow her to consort with him on school grounds, but occasionally I'd see them together at the Dairy Queen or at the bowling alley or just hanging around on the street, and often I was with Deanna when I saw him, and even then I pretended not to know him.

When the school term was over, Vance and his family moved away to New Jersey. Before he left he visited me while I was cleaning out my locker. He told me that he was leaving for good and wanted to say good-bye. He handed me a card with his new address and phone number on it. There was another number handwritten on the back of the card. Here, take this, Laugh Track, he said. Call me some time. It was good to know you. He flipped the card over and showed me the handwritten number. If you ever need help out of a jam, you can call this number. I thanked him and put the card in my wallet, and I keep it in my wallet to this day as a talisman, a marker from my vanished past.

I've never called him or the number on the back. I've never felt a need to use it, never been in the sort of jam that would require mob muscle. But sometimes, I do wonder who would answer the phone should I suddenly dial the handwritten number. Would it be some mob boss? Vance's docile girlfriend? Vance himself?

Besides these friends, my childhood was largely uneventful, save for the antagonism that daily grew between me and my brothers and father. The three of them formed an unbreakable triad cemented together by something akin to electromagnetic force. Like an H_2O molecule, they were nearly unbreakable and didn't easily admit a fourth atom. I was never allowed inside their clique. Hell, that would have produced heavy water. Retrospectively, it seems strange to me that a clique of men should form itself inside my family and that I should be excluded from it, but so it was.

I tried to be like my older brothers—to emulate them, to do the things I thought they wanted me to do—in order to enter into their tight circle. But I was invariably rebuffed. Such are the facts of my life. They have always seemed to me like action figures—distant, blurred, slightly misshapen—whom I peer at from the wrong end of a telescope. Maybe I'm the one who's to blame. Maybe it's me who's at the wrong end of the telescope. When they were young, they were always playing sports: hockey, baseball, football. As they grew older, they became fascinated with mechanical objects. All sorts of magazines like *Popular Mechanics* and how-to books suddenly descended on the house, including an obscure periodical called *Robert's Robot World* of only a few issues with cool illustrations of robots. They also collected parts manuals for old cars and motorcycles. My brothers really got into concocting mechanical things. They made robots out of found objects: PVC tubes, stroller wheels, lunchboxes, and electric motors culled from discarded erector sets. They'd set their robots to life with 12-volt batteries and have them combat each other. They'd give their robots simple meteorological names like Thunder, Wind, or Tornado. When one set of robots wore out, they'd go to work and produce a newer, stronger generation of robots. Thus they were always inventing, modifying, and enlarging their skill sets.

They were also into motorized vehicles at an early age. Their first motorized vehicles were minibikes that were powered by small two-stroke engines similar to ones found in lawn mowers. They would take off, the two of them, riding their minibikes down the street sidesaddle and at idle speed. When they reached the field, which had trails on it, they'd open their throttles and move fast over the bumpy dirt path, clouds of dirt and exhaust trailing in their wake. I used to stand at the edge of the field and watch them go. Milkweeds with their horn-shaped seedpods would rise to my chest, and all sorts of yellow and white butterflies, thick-bodied bumblebees, and yellow jackets would fly about in the air. I would stand and watch, and there my brothers were, off in the distance, driving their minibikes at full throttle. It looked fun as hell, and I wished I could do it with them, but for some reason, my father never let me have a minibike. You're too small, he would tell me. When I was old enough to ride a minibike, he told me, You're too injury prone. If you should fall off, you would kill yourself. My brothers took their cue from my old man. When I asked if I could ride on the back of their minibikes, they would refuse for fear I would burn my legs on the exhaust pipe. Their concern for me, in such moments, was merely veiled condescension, and I wasn't stupid enough to see it any other way, especially since they never shied away from letting their friends ride tandem with them.

As my brothers grew older, I watched them graduate to swifter, more powerful bikes. One year they both received enduro motorcycles for their birthdays, whereas I received . . . Well, I don't remember what. By the time they were teenagers, they each had full-sized motorcycles. My brother Sid rode a 500cc Yamaha off-road motorcycle; my other brother, Greg, rode a Honda 750cc Nighthawk street bike. My father, by the way, liked to fix old Mercedes Benzes and drive them to 500,000 miles. The three of them would spend all of their free hours working in the garage on their vehicles, newspapers spread out beneath them, oilcans, wrenches, socket sets, jars of screws and bolts scattered like surgical equipment, easily at hand. My father was constantly watching their progress, teaching them how to remove the engines from their bikes, showing them how to disassemble them completely, then reassemble them. Because, my father used to patiently explain to them, if you don't know your bikes from the inside out, you'll never be one with your bikes.

My brother Sid was more mechanically gifted than Greg. But Greg was self-assured, and he had other talents—a mathematical mind, a highly retentive and detail-oriented memory—that Sid couldn't match, so there was very little strife between them. Indeed, they've always been harmonious when working together, and, to this day, their ability to work together has produced tremendous results for the family business.

EVEN THOUGH I TRIED, I could never be naturally interested in any of the things my brothers and father did.
I didn't like sports or the tediousness of vehicles. The
whole concept of spending enormous amounts of time
and money on vehicles or sports was deeply repellent
to me. What's more, time has done nothing to reverse
this situation and make it better. Whenever I'm home for
a visit and listen to them talk among themselves—in a
sort of virile, hopped-up, masculine fashion—I feel like
a perpetual outsider. In truth, they bore me to tears. It's
as if they speak in a coded language, which, for years, I
felt under pressure to try and understand, but recently—
because I no longer care—I've given up trying. Truth be
told, they too have given up on me—dismissed me, is
more the word. They think I'm useless, without direction, without motivation. It's impossible for them to believe that I refuse to join the family business, never mind
that I've never been asked to go into it! If I had talents
(and they would never admit that I do), they'd accuse me
of squandering them. They also know about my uncle's
handouts, and these handouts have done an enormous
amount of damage to our relationships. My brothers
think I'm a fool for accepting them, and the fact that
my uncle hasn't sent them so much as a letter has given
them an opportunity to feel morally superior to me.

You'll be beholden to him, my oldest brother likes to
warn whenever he can. His money will take the teeth out
of your bite.

What do you mean?

Listen, my brother would say. It's like this: in order to
be a success in this world, you must be hungry. Uncle
Eddie, by sending you this money, is effectively keep-

ing you from feeling hunger in the pit of your stomach. But that's what you need—hunger! Hunger! My brother made a fist and pounded his abdomen for emphasis. Think of it this way, Gideon: he's keeping you from taking your diapers off or from riding your bike without training wheels. He's protecting you at a time of life when you need least to be protected. Do you really want to grow dependent on Uncle Eddie's handouts?

It sounds fine to me, I said, irritated by the reasonableness of my brother's observation. And what about you? I asked. All of your life, you and Sid have received handouts from Dad, and I didn't get a damned thing.

You're exaggerating, he said. You got plenty.

I laughed with disbelief. You've got to be kidding.

At which point my brother waived his hand at me in dismissal. Leave me alone. I feel truly sorry for you. He shook his head. You're a loser, and you have no excuse.

PERHAPS HE'S RIGHT: I have no excuse. However, I don't want to be excused for anything. I like my life just the way it is, and I wouldn't change it for anything. Nevertheless, I can't stand hypocrites, and my brothers fall into that category. Even though they pretend to be puritans (which they're not—they're Catholics) by always emphasizing the virtue of self-reliance, nevertheless, they have been among the last people to be truly self-reliant. My father inherited his business from my grandfather, and my brothers are in the process of inheriting the business from my dad. The truly self-reliant person in our family is my grandfather who had the balls to actually go out there and start his own business from scratch—no help from nobody, thank you very much.

I'm not saying I'm self-reliant, either; I don't pretend to be. But what my brothers fail to see, at least when it comes to my uncle's handouts, is that they haven't needed his handouts because my father has been generously funding each of them since the day he was born and that no one, other than my mother, has ever made an attempt to understand or help me, and when my uncle came along and saw the situation for what it was—when he first saw on the weekend he became my godfather—that it was them against me, he took it upon himself in a very quiet way to right what was wrong. These checks have become his way to establish balance and equality between me and them.

My uncle's checks came and went as did the days. One day flying into another and so many of those days spent drinking at the bar. And waiting. The door to the bar would fly open, and I'd turn my head to see who it was, who was coming in. If it was the face of one of the regulars, I turned my head back to my beer. If it was a new face, I stared at it, trying to figure it out. Who did it belong to, and why were they stopping in here? Sometimes someone walking through the bar might notice me and step up and say hello. They'd stay a moment or a few hours, and then they too would be gone to pursue their life, and I would never hear from them again. So many people were so busy. It was perplexing to me how one came to have so many plans, how one came to be so busy, always off doing something or another. For me, I have always felt a tremendous inertia. Whenever I felt motivated to do something, which was rarer and rarer the older I got, the more pointless it seemed. Why bother? I would say to myself. What's the point? And so I sat and I sat an awful long time not doing a damned thing. And so it went for a long time, and then, one day, something happened that changed everything.

I WAS TIRED FROM a night of poor sleep. I was in my car driving, flipping through stations on the radio wondering whatever would become of me. It was one of those bright, clear days. I was going about my business, going through the motions, running my errands and not paying enough attention to the world around me when someone driving a silver minivan through the intersection missed his red light. We were both moving fast, and in a careening instant we both skidded to avoid a high-impact collision. I realized quite calmly that I was on the cusp of being killed—a split second from death. Thankfully, the other driver must have had the same revelation. I could see it in his eyes in the slowed-down moment before the crash. (They were blue eyes, slightly haggard. Perhaps he too had had a poor night of sleep.) We both turned to get out of the way, and by the grace of god or good fortune we avoided each other, a narrow miss. Without so much as stopping we went on our ways, unscathed. But as I drove along, the shock of what I'd just narrowly missed was so overwhelming that I had to pull over to the side of the road and catch my breath. My hands were trembling, and I could feel my heart pounding.

Suppose I died, I thought to myself, sitting in my car. Who would care that I died? There was a moment there where I wasn't even sure I would care if I died. It might be easier to let all this go . . . But then something in me wanted there to be others who cared if I died. At the very least I wanted a small list of people who possibly might mourn my passing, a group of people who therefore cared that I had been part of their lives.

I could count on Victor, I thought, if I had to. He was my friend, my confidant, my mentor. He would definitely care if I suddenly died. He might even feel partly to blame for my death. I could probably count on Walt too. He might mourn my passing. He might even bury me in

Oak Woods Cemetery even though I vowed never to let Boettcher get his hands on me. He'd help the mourners out at the water bubbler. He'd help with the little orange flags on the cars. He'd dig the hole, lower me down, and fill the hole with a backhoe after the funeralgoers had departed. He might even be good enough to tend my grave through the seasons: dust the snow off my tombstone in the winter, plant flowers in the spring, pull weeds in the summer, and tidy it up in the fall.

My passing would likely crush my mother. She was already so weak and frail and haunted by a life that had never let her open her wings and fly. If I died it would ruin the rest of her days and plunge her into grief, and she would likely blame my death on my early unwillingness to attend birthday parties when I was a child and of course she would blame herself.

As for my father and my brothers, they might go through the motions of mourning, but let's face it: they wrote me off long ago, and for all intents and purposes I was already dead to them.

There weren't many others whom I could think of. I'm certain my uncle would care—but, frankly, in so many ways we never really knew each other. I was just someone he sent checks to. On the other hand, I knew about him, and he knew about me, and that must count for something. His wife, Nan, certainly wouldn't care that I died. In fact, she'd probably say I got what I deserved, and she'd likely be glad that now a line item could be removed from their budget.

As I sat there in my car, I couldn't think of any others who would care. I was a stranger to the rest of the world as the world was strange and overwhelming to me, and

so it would be a sparsely attended funeral. It was a sign—
a sad sign—that I hadn't worked hard enough inter-
braiding my life with the lives of others. Then I realized
that Claire would care if I died. In fact, I was convinced
that she would care. She might even come back to Chicago for the funeral and arrange the whole measly affair.
She might try and spruce it up and make it seem grander
than it was. She might even have some good things to say
about me in a eulogy—how she saw something good in
me from the very first, etcetera. Then she would help my
grieving mother situate herself, and Claire would likely
explain me to my brothers and my father, telling them
they never got who I was, and then she would be gone to
New York where, on the return flight home, she would
suddenly break down and cry, and then she would pull
herself together. And that would be that. I can even hear
her say to her friends, Such a waste of talent. It's so sad.

While I was having these thoughts I looked at myself
in the rearview mirror, and I realized I loved Claire and
I missed her and I wanted to get back into her life.

With Claire I never felt the need to apologize or confess because she did not judge me. She understood me.
From the first moment we met in the coffee shop, she
made me laugh, and then, with magic, she touched my
foot with hers, and I felt a release from the melancholy
of a lifetime. I had been born into the wrong family perhaps, and I had grown up with the wrong friends, and I
didn't fit in not because I didn't want to fit in but because
I never felt a common attachment to those in my milieu,
but I felt that attachment with Claire, and with that, I
started to feel better.

On a short list of indispensable people, she was at the

top. I would write a letter to Claire to see if her offer to come to New York was still good.

THAT EVENING I WENT to the bar, which was empty, and had a drink with Victor, and I asked him, I said: I turn to you for all fatally important advice.

He lifted his brandy and clinked it to mine.

You know I'm getting older. I may not always be here for you.

But I was wondering—when you say the world beckons, what do you mean by that?

I mean the world is your oyster is what I mean. Get out of this place and go become a part of it. You're too young to rot in a place like this. You've got so much good in you to offer the world.

But, Victor, when you say the world beckons, can it also be that someone is calling you? I mean, if someone sees something in you, and you see something in them, is that the beckoning you're talking about as well?

Yes. It can mean that too. Victor paused. Did you find someone?

I did awhile back, but I think today I learned a long-delayed lesson.

And what was that?

That I had been putting off a person who in my heart I really always loved.

You only discovered that now?

I discovered it today. I don't know what took me so damn long. I've taken too many things for granted—and I treated her poorly before she left. I now wish I hadn't.

Do I know this person?

Claire. She too has told me not to rot in this place.

Then she's a good person. You should listen to her. In fact, take my advice, son. Don't waste time. Try to get her back before it's too late.

She's already left for New York, and I don't want to leave this place. I like it here. I like you. This is home.

Listen, you can make your home anywhere. It doesn't need to be this place. Go to New York if you must—if that's what she wants—and then work it out from there. Who knows, you might even be happy in New York and never think twice about this place or me again. But go. Be happy with her. That is, if she'll take you back.

What do you mean? And leave you?

I'll always take you back, but it's time for you to go and find your own way.

He raised his glass and smiled at me. He put his hand on mine, and I thanked him.

Prost, Victor, I said.

Happiness, he said back.

Long life, I said.

Happy life.

THAT NIGHT WHEN I returned home, I wrote a note to Claire.

> Dear Claire,
>
> I don't expect a woman like you to take a person like me back. But I think you understand me. You always have understood me. You understood me somehow on the day we first met at that coffee shop, and you understood me on the steps of the library when you told me that I had the ideas and the ambition to do something with my life, and you

understood who I was when I told you to go back to New York without me. I don't understand why you chose me of all people, and I never will. You were not wrong in seeing what was good in me, and you would not be wrong to keep in mind how horribly I have treated you. I'm a slow starter is all, and I think you know that about me. It has taken me time to understand the consequential things in life, and there aren't too many consequential things that I can think of outside of you. I was slow to admit to either of us what I've known all along—that I love you and that I want to be with you wherever you are if you'll take me back . . .

I've placed bets on long shots many times, and I only won once on a lame horse that somehow found the guts to outrun the others in the final stretch. I will be that horse for you if you take me back. I promise.

Love, Gideon

I woke up early the next morning to mail the letter. Then I walked east to the lake. I didn't know if my letter was a good idea or a colossally stupid idea, whether indeed I would be able to be her winning horse, lame though I was, or whether, before long, I determined that my instincts were correct to stay in my hole and rot—but I was game at least to find out.

At Promontory Point there stood that man facing the rising sun, moving his body, doing his tai chi, and I stood near him mimicking his gestures, trying to learn. When he turned to me, I introduced myself, and we shook hands, and he said: Look here, my friend, this is how you do it. And I followed him while the sun raised its lionlike head over the blue and gorgeous waters of the lake. In a moment I was holding my arms outstretched on either side as if I were weighing my idea to try again with Claire. It seemed a weightless and ephemeral idea, and with it I felt as if I were slowly . . . floating away.

The change came a few weeks later when two notes arrived in the mail on the same day—the last Wednesday of the month. The first was in Claire's handwriting, and the other was in a hand I did not know. I opened Claire's first. Inside was a postcard with the image of a gigantic carved foot from the Colossus of Constantine. In a looping scrawl she wrote:

> My dear Gideon, You really put your big foot in your mouth, didn't you? Telling me to go on my way . . . I was wondering when you would finally figure it out. I'm traveling in Europe till the end of the month. Then I will be in Manhattan where you know how to find me. I expect you with roses in hand and an apology on the fifteenth of next month. I still have an instinct on us. Until then, sow the last of your wild oats at the track with Walt and in that old bar of yours, and figure out how to pack.
> Love, Claire
> P.S.: If you want to make umbrellas or anything else having to do with spring flowers, I will make the rain.

I opened the second envelope. It didn't contain a check, and the letter was written in a heavy, broken script by Nan. It merely said:

> He's had a stroke. Come soon.

Included in the letter were directions to his hospital in Fort Lauderdale. I caught a plane out of Midway the next day, and by three o'clock in the afternoon, with a cool Atlantic breeze blowing through the palm trees and seagulls drifting inland on a high wind with their narrow wings etched white against the brilliant blue sky, I was dropped off at the hospital entrance by a cab. I took the elevator up, and I was directed by nurses at the station where to find him. I entered his room, and there my benefactor lay on a bed partly hidden by a curtain. I pushed the curtain aside and walked over to him.

Hey, Unc. I touched him on the shoulder to wake him up.

He was wheezing through his oxygen tube. He was ninety-two, and I was twenty-eight. He opened his eyes, and I saw his lips move. I think I heard him say something, but I couldn't make it out. I asked him ever so politely to say it again.

What's that, Unc?

The plan . . . did you bring your plan?

I held his hand. It was cold and dry. He was bony, a sack of skin that was flaking. My immediate reaction was to make up something, but it was too late for that.

Your plan, he breathed again, barely audible.

I don't have a plan just yet, Unc, but I think I might have found a girl. . . . Her name is Claire. You would like her. I promise you that. I'm likely to move to New York City to be with her. I'll need to give you my new address so you can write me when they bust you out of this place.

I took everything in with my eyes—the flickering technology that kept him alive, the tropical sun beating against the louvered shades—then I looked at him.

There was a long pause. He seemed to be collecting himself. Then he said, That's a good . . . plan.

He abruptly clutched my hand in his. I think he smiled a little. Who can say? He was on that damned respirator. His face was a mask, and the look on his face was the look of a man who, dangling from a cliff by his fingers, desperately wanted to hang on. And then he let go, and I saw him fall until his eyes went blank.